A Full Moon in August

By Joseph H. Randolph

Cover designed by, Ivory Garlock

V:4

ISBN: 979-8354700639 (Paperback)

For my father, George the Barber

A Full Moon in August

By Joseph H. Randolph

Chapter 1 (Thomas)

Friday August 14, 1981 -- 4:00 pm EST - Toronto

I needed *something.* I couldn't quite put my finger on it. I had a craving for change; I needed something extraordinary to happen because, until now, life was boring, *very* boring, in fact.

There I was at the age of twenty-one, about to travel on a solo journey from Toronto to Vancouver. It was a trip I had planned weeks ago—I just needed to get away from home. I took the window seat facing west while the train waited for the last of the passengers to board. With the doors still open, I rested my head against the expansive section of glass, it was smooth and cool to the touch. Even though there weren't many people on the train, it was still fairly populated considering each section had already been claimed by the time I occupied the last available spot. *Maybe if I'm lucky enough, I'll be able to stretch out my legs and not have to share this section with anyone else.*

I stared out the window, observing passengers scurrying back and forth on the platform. In the background, I heard a distant, mumbled voice over the speaker system announcing the departure of various trains from their respective podiums.

My train was due to leave and just as I was expecting to get the entire section to myself, a man bolted onto the platform, carrying a suitcase. I watched as he scanned the length of the train, deciding upon which car to enter.

Not mine. Not mine. Please, not mine.

He turned awkwardly back to the station as if someone had called him, he stood silently for a moment then rushed towards the door to my car. He noisily boarded; the clunking of his uneasy steps annoyed me immensely. He stopped close by and glanced toward the section I was in.

“Excuse me...” he said breathlessly before I silently retracted my stretched-out legs to let him through.

Shit! Oh well. I huffed out loud. *So much for that!*

With a tired sigh, he plopped himself into the seat across from me. It didn't take long for him to start shifting uncomfortably, incessantly peering down at his seat as if something were caught between his pants and the cushion. He twisted his neck toward the aisle and made a feeble attempt to peek over the back of his seat with no success. I watched suspiciously. His frantic behavior paused for a moment, allowing him to rub his hands together as if to stay warm, albeit it wasn’t cold on the train. Moments later, he stared out the window, straining his neck as far as he could, as his eyes searched in either direction along the platform—his movements were jerky and agitated. It was a little unsettling. Eventually, he put his frenzied behavior to a halt and fell back in his seat and let out another sigh before relaxing his neck, seemingly fatigued from the search.

After getting over the fact that I wouldn't have my privacy, I thought about that man across from me who just boarded. *Is this just going to be another dull passenger who would eventually talk my ear off while I pretend to be engaged? Or . . . maybe this guy has something going on? Yeah... I think he does. Let's do it, Tommy-boy. Let's turn the tables and dig into this dude. Rather than have him initiate conversation, maybe I'll get the ball rolling. Perhaps he's got secrets. Maybe he's done something atrocious, something truly unforgivable. Yeah. Let's plug into this one. I'll need the entertainment, anyway. I'm tired of the same ol' Tommy routine.*

Suddenly the man slid his suitcase underneath his seat in haste, banging the corners of it on the posts below. Just as he lifted his head, his eyes met mine. He nodded, but I betrayed myself and turned away just as he did. It made me feel childish. *Damn! I already failed.* From the corner of my eye, I noticed him peering out the window again. He was straining less this time. I slowly brought my line of sight back to have a better look at him. He was a middle-aged man with dark brown hair that was slickly combed back with very distinct white poking through. His complexion was a rich olive and he had a Frenchman's nose. He had a European look about him, but it wasn't a typical southern or northern European look. With his strong jawline on a rather small face, he reminded me of an actor I once saw in a foreign movie.

The doors closed and an announcement over the train's speaker system declared that the train would be departing; its first stop—Sudbury Junction. After a couple of minutes, the train jerked forward. I turned back to peer out the window, but from the corner of my eye, I noticed the man looking down at his hands. He brought them together, touching the pads of his palms and rubbing them as he did earlier. He closed his eyes and rested. With his head angled back, his jawline was stretched so tight that his skin revealed the green and blue colored arteries in his neck. At a quick glance you would think he was dead. He tilted his head to one side while his eyes remained closed, placing his head on his left hand to keep it stable. I watched curiously as he shifted a few times before he settled into a final position.

As the train slowly gained speed, the passenger car rocked haphazardly from side to side– forcing my body to slant with it. The man across from me moved with it too, but I could tell he wasn't asleep, as his body was tense and rigid. I found the distant squeal of the train's wheels echoing against the tall buildings haunting. The rapid *clickety-clack* of the train speeding along its tracks was bothersome at first, but after some time I got used to it, which allowed my mind to rest so that I could close my eyes. But every time I did, I would open them suddenly for fear that I might miss out on what the man across from me and what he could possibly do next. *What is it about him? Something was going on with this guy. Something was weighing on his mind. Or . . . maybe my intuition is wrong. I'm probably reading into it too much.*

I removed my jacket and crumpled it up against the side window with the intent of getting some rest. But just as I was about to close my eyes, I noticed the slits of the man's eyes open ever-so-slightly and close again. At first I squinted at him, but then I eventually shut mine. I began to think about my family but that made me homesick, so I let my mind wonder about random thoughts such as what my first car would be or what kind of career I might fall into. Although I was only twenty-one, I hadn't really accomplished anything of significance. This was the first trip I'd taken and I had decided to skip school that year with the intent of enrolling into something in the following year—but into what exactly? I wasn't quite sure.

The train shifted abruptly, causing my head to lift away from the window and my jacket to fall to the floor. When I leaned to pick it up and place it on the seat beside me, I discovered that the man across from me was sitting up straight, looking out the window. His demeanor was much different from the last time we were both awake and alert. He was relaxed. *This guy's not that interesting after all.* I sat up and turned my neck to have a peak out of the windows across the train car and then out of my own. *Oh well. So much for my experiment.* Pole after pole, tree after tree, small town after small town—for miles and miles. The landscape stretched endlessly with different colors and hues—lush greenery to vibrant blue lakes. Each town flashed by with its passing scenery. I found the blobs of color passing by me uninteresting and it eventually made me nauseous, so I pulled out a book that I'd swiftly grabbed before I left. It was a copy of *A Farewell to Arms*, a book I managed to steer clear of during high school yet oddly found at home. I set the book beside my jacket.

"*A Farewell to Arms*. Now, that's a good book!" said the man across from me. His eyes flickered from the dog-eared copy to me. *He was talking to me*. "Which part are you at?" He inquired, breaking the quiet hum of the train again. I looked up, momentarily taken aback by the sudden interest. He seemed like the kind of guy that would keep to himself when it came to strangers.

"I haven't started it yet," I admitted with a tinge of anticipation. "I thought I would get a chance on this long train ride."

The man turned to watch the strong afternoon sun pierce through the windows. Along the south side of the train, the bright light reflected off of his face as the sun danced through the tall and mighty spruce trees.

"I read that book for the first time when *I* was a young man."

He stared at me as if waiting for a reply, his unwavering gaze making me shift uncomfortably. He didn't blink, and I found myself looking away briefly in unease. I can't say what it was about his ability to maintain his gaze, but I was almost overwhelmed by it as if it had some type of control over me. It reminded me of one of my old high school teachers. It was uncomfortable, but it also created curiosity at the same time.

"How old are you?" he demanded, his tone sharp and direct.

"Twenty-one, "I replied with a silent gulp.

"Yeah. I read it at about the same time." He paused. "No, I think I was a little older," he said, turning to look out the north side of the train. "It's an old book. Written in the nineteen-twenties, I believe. Hemmingway uses the word 'darling' a lot, which you'll have to get used to." He turned to face me again. "It's a war-time love story situated in Italy during WWI. The love story . . . well, I didn't quite get it at the time." He was about to say something else but stopped and turned his head back to study my reaction. "Don't worry," he reassured, a sly smile playing on his lips. "I won't give it away."

I peered down at the book to avoid his unwavering stare. I flipped through it to give him the impression I was about to read it, but I didn't want to. Not yet. I was too preoccupied with *him. Maybe my first intuition was correct. Ok. Let's try this again.* "Are you going to Vancouver too?" I managed to spit out.

I made eye contact with him again and he began to look down at the book spread out on my lap, then back up at me.

"Yes and no. I'll arrive in Vancouver, then rent a car and drive it to Victoria."

"Are you going back home?"

The left side of his lips lifted forming a suspicious grin.

"What makes you think I'm going back home?"

I couldn't read his demeanor. I was nervous.

"I don't know." My shoulders lifted. "Just a guess," I said feeling embarrassed.

"Actually . . . you're right! My mother isn't well. I need to spend some time with her. She's getting on in years."

I sat silently as he studied the passing trees, wondering what was going through his mind. He sat rigid, unable to relax and he kept shifting in his seat. His posture was tense—holding some type of stress. *Yes. Something was troubling him.*

"And you?" the man asked, turning back around rather suddenly. "Where are you off to?"

"I'm going to see a childhood friend who moved to Vancouver." I paused for a moment. "This is my first big trip away from home." I immediately felt a pang of self-consciousness, berating myself for the awkward way it came out. My cheeks warmed with embarrassment as I wished I could retract my words.

"Good for you!" He exclaimed. "One should travel while still young. Go to Europe if you can. You'll get a different perspective of what life is really like. Not only that, but the culture and history, if you're into that of course." He paused and his gaze was fixated on me. "How old did you say you were?"

“Twenty-one.”

“Man . . . if I were only twenty-one again. The things I would do . . . and do differently.” He sighed again. “Don’t make the . . .” He abruptly stopped. The man made a quick turn towards the center aisle, checking his surroundings, and then he leaned forward. He waved me towards him and followed the gesture with a whisper, “Listen. Can you do something for me?” The sudden change in his demeanor caught me off guard, but curiosity sparked within me.

"OK..." I replied, my interest piqued by the unexpected turn in our interaction.

“Can you get up, you know, casually . . . stretch or something and then walk up and down the car,” he urged, his voice tinged with an unsettling urgency. “I want you to see if there is a bald-headed man with a dark beard. He’s a . . .” He flexed his shoulders and arms, “. . . a husky sort of guy.”

I studied the man’s face before answering. His eyes held the same intensity as they did earlier. Upon a closer look, they appeared frightful and bloodshot. Although it was unusual for me, I suppressed any hesitation. “OK,” I replied, standing and began my theatrics.

It was weird, but I kind of enjoyed the task. It was like a silly dare I played in high school. With the man gazing up at me while I left our section to pace the car, I casually searched each section as I strode westbound and, after another stretch, turned back and continued eastbound.

As I began to stroll down the aisle, some of the passengers peeped up at me peculiarly. Their eyes followed my casual moves before going back to themselves. It added an extra layer of tension to the atmosphere of the train car.

After my suspicious-looking stroll, I sat back in my seat and leaned toward the man. Part of me wanted to lie and say yes to see what kind of reaction I would get, but I decided to be honest with him. "I don't see a man with that description."

"Good." He murmured, his nod slow and deliberate, and he rubbed his hands together.

He rested his head back against his seat and slouched down slightly. Perhaps I was being naïve but I fully expected him to divulge what that exercise was all about, but he didn't. He remained silent and less tense than before.

I sat perfectly still, watching this grown man's body become supple as if the air was being let out of a tire bit by bit. He didn't seem to be in the mood to talk any longer, so I picked up my book and began to read about Lt. Fredric Henry and his friend Rinaldi.

7:30 pm

(Somewhere between Toronto and Sudbury Junction)

After what felt like several hours, I looked up from my book; the man's head was bent back, his eyes shut, and his mouth was partially open. He was definitely asleep this time, as his body was completely relaxed and swaying with the train car as it jerked side to side. His hands wiggled on his lap as if they were made of rubber; they appeared older than they should. I could not read the man at all while he slept, his features remained inscrutable and enveloped in mystery even in slumber—something that struck me as peculiar.

I knew it was selfish of me but I couldn't help it; I found myself desperate for a distraction and he was the closest thing to one. I wanted it! I even considered banging my foot to wake him, but my compassion for the disturbed man took over. It was a morbid curiosity and I surprised myself by indulging in it. I knew the man was a wreck and I had a craving for more.

I tried to carry on reading about Lt. Fredric Henry and his love for Catherine Barkley for a while, but I kept peering up at the man, hoping he would wake so that I could read *him* and not that book. I placed the novel back on my lap and continued my examination of the man until he let out a sudden snort, jolting him awake with a disoriented look crossing his face as he sat up. His eyes scanned me and the seats around us. I turned away as I'm sure he didn't know where he was for the first few seconds. He cleared his throat and ran his nimble fingers through his hair, acting as if nothing happened; perhaps he was recalling the images of whatever dream still lingered in his mind, replaying scenes that had left their mark. His conscious state was much more dynamic than his sleep state. I noticed that there was little movement of his eyebrows, but his eyeballs seemed to drill into you if you made contact with them. They were an open invitation to engage with him.

"The sun's starting to go down," the man said gruffly. "Do you like nighttime? Are you a night owl?" He tilted his head slightly, rubbing his eyes to get the sleepiness out of them.

Before I could answer, he continued.

"I don't care for it myself. That's why I hate wintertime. Daytime is so short. It's dark and desolate." He paused, his voice carrying a trace of bitterness. "Even as a child, I remember sitting in my bedroom, listening to the winter wind howling through the old windows. You know that sound the wind makes? That 'woooooooooOOOOoo' sound," he mocked. "As if there were ghosts hovering just outside your bedroom window. I hated it!" His eyes had glazed over and he crossed his arms, seemingly lost in the conversation. "You know." He chuckled to himself while looking at me. "I was a bit of a baby, even in my early adolescence. I needed my mother's soothing voice before I could fall asleep." His face softened as he said, "But even in my early twenties, I . . ." He closed his mouth and turned to me. "I'm sorry, I've been rambling. I'm taking you away from your book."

"I can read that anytime." I wanted to hear what was going on in this man's head. I wanted him to tell me about the bearded man, so I continued with the idle chit-chat. "I know that sound too."

"What sound?" he asked rather harshly.

"That howling sound the wind makes."

"Oh, yeah. Memories. Childish I suppose," he shrugged as he looked at his wristwatch, then out the window, then back to me. "What's your name?"

"Thomas."

"I'm Henry. Nice to meet you." He leaned forward to shake my hand.

He didn't talk much after our short chat and eventually fell back asleep, so I cracked open my book again.

11:15 pm

I woke to find Henry staring at me with his piercing eyes. The lights from the station pained my eyes as they shone through the train car windows. The wheels screeched as they came to a halt, disturbing the beautiful hum of the train's rapid movement along the tracks, which I became so accustomed to.

"Looks like we're at our first stop," he remarked, his eyes flicking down to his watch as he spoke. "It's quarter after eleven." Through my window, the platform began to slide into view. The train began to slow to a halt and the chug of the engine faded into a low hum.

The train car doors opened and a gust of fresh air filled the cabin. My arms began to fill with goosebumps as I waited for the doors to close. I could hear an announcement through the loud-speakers, listing all the stops ahead of us, which I didn't pay much attention to as I really just wanted to get to Vancouver—and that was still days away.

There wasn't much activity on the platform, but the train remained stationary with its doors open. The announcer had stopped his broadcast, which was overtaken by Roy Orbison's "*Mama.*"

The song played for barely a minute when Henry bent over abruptly, his movements were almost forceful as he placed his forearms on his lap and buried his face in his hands. I sat up, startled by the sudden shift in his demeanor. He seemed so vulnerable, and... delirious. His body trembled and, for a moment, I mistook it for aching laughter but I soon realized he was attempting to conceal his sobs. His sullen and waterlogged eyes peered up at me and I found myself unable to look away.

"Sorry." He tried to apologize and he sniffled. "It's been a little stressful lately." He reached into his pocket for a tissue and wiped his nose, then pushed the tears away with the palms of his hands.

I said nothing and I just continued to gawk.

He let out a long exhale followed by, "Woo! That came outta nowhere. Oh boy. The stupid things I . . ." He began to deflect his sudden outburst.

I leaned in as his voice faded and became inaudible, unable to hear the last of his sentence.

“What’s that?” I asked.

“Oh. That song. Brought back memories of an ex-girlfriend.” He looked away and his eyes began to water again, but his tears remained in his eyes this time.

I waited for a moment before picking up my book, flipping through the pages to give Henry his space, but it appeared he needed—or wanted—to engage.

"Do you have a girlfriend?" he asked.

"No," I replied simply, wondering where this conversation was leading.

"Oh, you will," he continued, a faint smile playing on his lips. "Just don’t mess it up like I did," he added, his voice tinged with regret as he stared into the distance.

Tell me. Spill your guts. What the hell happened to you to make you break down like that?

“What happened?”

"Ah..." he sighed, sitting up and waving dismissively. "You don’t want to know about my stupid love life. You’ve got your book."

I leaned in, intrigued. "Go ahead."

He hesitated, "Really? You wanna hear this?"

"Sure."

"It’s kind of a long story," he admitted with a chuckle, "And well . . . we’ve got loads of time."

I agreed, my leg shaking in anticipation.

"OK." He took a long breath in and exhaled. "I lived with a woman many years ago when I was twenty-five. I know this because I celebrated my twenty-fifth birthday just before meeting her. Anyway, her name was Angie Peterson."

The doors closed and shortly after, the train jerked ahead and off we went.

Chapter 2 (Henry)

Saturday August 15, 1981 -- 12:00 am EST – Sudbury Junction

Henry told the young man his story but left out many intimate details. Even though it was several years ago, the memory was still vivid. 'Hi, baby.' It was the sound of her voice that brought back all those memories.

The Story of Angie Peterson

"Hi, baby." Angie greeted him with a big hug.

"Come on in. Take your usual seat. I'll be right with you... Just need to add the spices," she said warmly, gesturing towards the kitchen as she shuffled off. The sound of her humming filled the air. The aroma of the tomato sauce was pleasing to her guest.

Henry was introduced to Angie at a party, where her bubbly personality immediately caught his attention. Though initially he had little interest in her, her vibrant energy quickly grew on him. She found him at a turbulent period in his life when he found himself in between jobs, his finances were dwindling. The pressure mounted as he struggled to keep up, including missing payments to his roommate for their shared rent. Not having the means to entertain his new girlfriend, he often found himself at her place.

Angie rented an old house in north Whitby that was in need of a lot of work but he still found it warm and cozy. The house's south windows were expansive which allowed its interior to be bathed in sunlight, filling the space with warmth and brightness. However, the view from the east was obscured by towering cedar trees.

While the radio played, Henry thumbed through a few copies of *The National Geographic* that were scattered about her coffee table. He hadn't eaten all day and the smell from her kitchen was causing his stomach to growl. Moments later, she walked around the couch, with a wooden spoon still in her hand.

"So . . . what's new?" She casually inquired, draping her legs over his lap and wrapping her arms around his shoulders, drawing him into her embrace.

Angie was a naturally beautiful girl with brown hair and brown eyes. She had full, pink lips that the young man enjoyed kissing. It wasn't just that though; no, it was her body language and her voice -- he found it silky and soothing. When she asked a simple question like "what's new?" She always tilted her head slightly. It was something he was always fond of.

"Nothing, really," he sighed. "I'm feeling a little discouraged by the fact I haven't found anything yet."

"Don't worry," she said, pushing his hair just above his eyes as his mother used to when he was little. "You'll find something soon." She kissed his forehead. When the song on the radio changed, it began with muted trumpets, which inspired the young woman to bounce on his lap after a few bars.

"I love this song!" Angie slapped her hand on his chest, still swaying, singing. "Someday, when I'm awfully low," she sang, holding the wooden spoon to her mouth, swinging her head side to side as she did. "When the world seems cold, I will feel a glow just thinking of you, and the way you look . . ." She stuck her finger into Henry's chest, ". . . tonight."

She ended the first verse with a kiss on the young man's lips.

It was moments like those which became special for the young man. He enjoyed her. He enjoyed her company, her caressing, and her genuine care for him. He hadn't had that before. He also hadn't made love with her until that day either.

That kiss led to many more and became deeper as the two squeezed each other tightly. Henry pulled up her shirt and shoved his hands down her jeans causing his host's body to rise. He could feel her hips gyrate as he grabbed and squeezed her cheeks.

"Mmmmmm...," she moaned, thrusting herself into his groin. The two held each other, exploring one another until she slowly pulled away and got off the couch.

She began to take off her clothes. She tossed her blue top onto the floor, her undergarments following, which she kicked carelessly under the coffee table in one fluid motion.

"Stand up!"

He did.

Henry watched as Angie confidently unbuckled his belt, which fell to the floor along with his pants and briefs.

She guided him back onto the sofa, skillfully removing his shirt with a devilish grin before stroking him.

Once ready, she took advantage of her achievement, positioning herself over top, letting herself down until she reached a perfect rhythm. As they indulged in the passionate sensations, Angie tilted her head back and closed her eyes in bliss. His remained open, enjoying the image and the sensation of her bare breasts brushing up against his chest.

Henry gently ran his fingers along her glistened back, then shifted his hands to her hips. He wished the moment would last longer, but he knew it would soon come to an end. However, he managed to hold on until Angie's gratified groan signaled her climax, allowing him to find release as well.

When the two had finished, his head fell onto her heaving chest where his hot breath expired onto her breasts; the salty moisture from her skin blessed his bottom lip. A warm, comforting sensation came over him, something he hadn't felt before. With other women, he would want to roll over, but not with Angie. He felt close to her. He recalled that moment, her face tucked into his neck, her hands lightly placed on his shoulders. It was truly beautiful.

"That was wonderful, baby!" she whispered.

Oh, that whisper. The whisper from her moist warm breath. For him, that was perfection. He could have died right there and been content with life, but he had to ruin it.

"Do you mind if I jump in the shower?" he asked. "I need to rinse off."

"Of course, baby. You're probably hungry, aren't you?"

"I'm famished!"

After dinner, the two cuddled on the couch while listening to the radio. She could barely keep her eyes open, so he walked her upstairs, where he lay on his back with his left arm around her shoulder, while she nestled into it, leaving her hand on his stomach. This was how she fell asleep. Within seconds, his new girlfriend breathed soft, wispy, blowing breaths, bringing a smile to the young man's face.

* * *

As time went on, Henry found himself spending more and more time at Angie's until it felt like he practically lived there. His main responsibilities included keeping the house tidy and having dinner ready for her when she returned home. One cherished routine they shared was their "beer exchange." Each day, Angie would bring home two bottles of beer, placing them in the refrigerator for the next day while enjoying the ones from the day before that were nice and cold. Like clockwork, she would shower and then they would sit together in the kitchen, sipping their beers and chatting about their day.

"Cheers, baby!" she chuckled, placing her cherub lips over the cool rim of the bottle.

As his interest grew in his new girlfriend, there were several nuances he hadn't noticed before, like her faint smile lines, the perfect angle of her eyebrows, and the fact that she wore very little makeup. She also had her cute quirks too, like when she would clear her throat before asking a serious question or would sing or hum "Walkin' After Midnight" every time she cooked.

With her foot playfully resting on his lap, still wrapped in her bathrobe, she looked at him expectantly. "So? What did you get up to today? Did you get out?" Her eyes sparkled with curiosity, eager to hear about his day.

"I did. I filled out an application at Vanhemman Tire and some automotive part shops in town." He intertwined his fingers together nervously. "Fingers crossed."

"Cheers to that!" she exclaimed, raising her bottle in a toast.

"What's going on at The Village Bake Shoppe?"

"Did I ever tell you about these two old ladies that frequent the place?"

He shook his head and took a swig of beer.

"They come in every afternoon at four," she began, "They order tea and strudel and gossip the entire time. They've been coming for years." She paused, a hint of bitterness creeping into her tone. "Well, today, I served them. They were really curt with me, and after I took their money, you know, to get their change, I could see them leaning in towards each other. I know they were talking about me."

Her brow furrowed as she recounted the encounter, her discomfort evident. She squinted slightly before clearing her throat, "Am I getting fat?"

"What? Where did that come from?" he asked, genuinely puzzled.

"They were talking about me, that's for sure!" she exclaimed in frustration. "My pants have been getting tight lately."

"Don't be silly," he reassured her, reaching out to gently squeeze her hand. "They're just a couple of old biddies with nothing better to do than complain."

"Thanks, baby," she murmured, a small smile tugging at the corners of her lips.

* * *

Henry woke the next morning in a slight daze. He sat up for a moment, wondering what day it was. He didn't even hear his girlfriend leave, but recalled the kiss on the cheek and took in the fragrance of her perfume that still lingered in the room.

He rose from the bed and stumbled down the stairs, still feeling groggy. Filling the percolator with water and adding ground coffee to the top, he placed it on the stove. Taking a seat at the kitchen table, he glanced at a note left for him:

Good morning, handsome! It's going to be a beautiful day today. Get out and get some fresh air! Don't worry about dinner, I'll make sandwiches for us tonight.

Love,

Angie

After his coffee he showered, dressed, and strolled along the dirt road toward the bus stop. He'd slept longer than he had thought, and by the time he made it to the corner, it was already lunchtime. The number nineteen bus took him into town and stopped at Byron Street. He walked along the main road to the lake and sat on a bench for several hours, watching young mothers walk along the boardwalk with their little ones.

Although the late summer sun was warm, the breeze off the lake was cool, so he put his jacket back on.

"Hey Mister," a boy's voice called out from behind, breaking Henry's reverie.

Turning around, Henry faced the boy with a small smile. "Hi there."

"What ya doing?" the boy asked, squinting one eye in curiosity.

"Ummm... just taking in the day," Henry replied, gesturing to the surroundings.

"Why aren't ya working?"

Henry hesitated, then replied, "Listen, kid, don't you have something to do?" He immediately regretted his curt response upon seeing the boy's saddened expression. Realizing the boy was alone, he softened his tone and added, "It's my day off."

"Okay, mister. Wanna throw the ball with me?" the boy asked eagerly, holding out his baseball glove and ball.

"Sure! Why not!"

Getting up from his spot, Henry walked a few paces toward the lake before turning around to face the boy.

"Go ahead. Remember, I don't have a padded glove like you do."

Undeterred, the boy did his wind-up and threw the ball high into the air, watching with delight as it descended into Henry's open hands. Henry tossed it back, marveling at the boy's accuracy as he safely caught it with his gloved hand. They repeated this simple exchange for about twenty minutes.

"Okay, kid. My arm's getting sore," Henry finally admitted, feeling a twinge of fatigue.

"Okay, mister," the boy replied, his disappointment evident as he hung his head and started to walk away.

"Hey!" Henry called out.

"Yeah?" The boy turned back.

"You've got a great arm. Keep practicing!"

"Okay. Thanks, mister."

Henry plopped himself back on the bench and watched the boy stroll carelessly along the side of the road.

The unemployed man sat on the bench for another hour, taking in the fresh air. He was in no rush to head home to those all-too-familiar four walls but eventually got up and took a different route back to the bus stop, which entailed taking a narrow street dotted with large walnut trees on either side; its fruit left stains on the concrete sidewalk as he strode past. At the end of the street was a small coffee shop and the fresh aromas from it lured him in. He took a seat on one of the round, padded stools along the counter, placing his elbows on top.

"Hi, honey." A woman with large blonde hair was wiping the counter. "What can I get ya?" She chewed bubble gum, her jaw moving, and her mouth opening and closing as she did. While she waited for Henry to answer, the young man couldn't help but notice her heavily painted blue and green eye shadow, which was ever so present when she batted her eyes.

"A cup of coffee and a slice of pie. What do you recommend?" Henry asked, scanning the wall menu with interest.

"Oh, sweetie, you gotta have the lemon meringue."

"Lemon meringue it is!"

At the other end of the curved countertop, sat a man with salt and pepper hair and a mustache; His demeanor was somehow unsettling. He took deliberate puffs of his cigarette like a pipe and the smoke curled around him. He was probably a war vet, Henry concluded. As Henry stole glances in his direction, he also noticed that the man had been studying him since he arrived. Despite his best efforts to ignore him, Henry's curiosity got the better of him, causing him to look over, which he quickly regretted.

"The pie's good here," the man said with a gravelly voice.

"Here ya go, honey." The waitress placed his coffee on the counter, causing it to spill slightly. He wiped the bottom of it with a napkin, added some sugar, and raised his cup to the vet.

"I will let you know what I think," Henry eventually mumbled, his voice barely audible above the din of the diner.

The war vet grumbled something under his breath, his expression inscrutable.

"And there's your pie. Enjoy!" The waitress set the lemon meringue pie in front of Henry, its vibrant yellow filling and fluffy whipped cream enticingly beckoning.

"Thanks," Henry replied, offering the waitress a polite smile before turning his attention to his dessert.

As he reached across the counter to grab a newspaper and scan the headlines, Henry found himself continuously distracted by the war vet. The man's gaze seemed to bore into him, his eyes following Henry's every move. The small and deliberate puffs of smoke that emitted curled in the air like tendrils of mist. Despite his attempts to focus on the newspaper, Henry couldn't shake the feeling of unease that settled over him in the war vet's presence.

"You new in town?" the vet quipped.

Henry slowly turned to observe the man, noting the way he held his cigarette between his yellowed thumb and index finger. "Pardon me?" Henry replied, slightly taken aback by the abruptness of the man's question.

"I said," the vet repeated harshly. "Are you new in town?"

"Kind of. Yes. I moved in with my girlfriend a few weeks ago," Henry replied.

"Is that so?" the vet mused, his gaze piercing. "You don't believe in marriage first?"

Henry paused, considering the question carefully before responding. "No. I suppose I don't," he replied, turning his attention back to his newspaper.

"Back in my day," the vet continued. "You proposed marriage, tied the knot..." He took another puff of his cigarette, the ember glowing brightly in the dimly lit diner. "...and then you moved in together. Kids nowadays. They got it all ass-backward if you ask me."

"No one's asking," Henry replied tersely as he glanced back at the man.

"Hey! There's no need for that!" the vet retorted, his voice sharp with indignation. "I'm just talking to you, is all."

Henry didn't respond, while the veteran sat silent, puffing away on what remained of his cigarette. Henry was a little agitated but remained seated and felt proud of himself for holding his ground. When it came time to finish his pie, he enjoyed his coffee, sipping it slowly rather than rushing out as he had originally planned.

Casually strolling to the bus stop, Henry thought about what the man at the coffee shop said. He realized for the first time that marriage was likely the next step. *What's going through her mind? Is she thinking about marriage already? Is she expecting me to propose?*

* * *

When he returned, his girlfriend was already home.

"Well, hello. Where did you wander off to today?" Angie asked as the young man passed through the door.

"What? No 'Hi baby'?"

"Hello, baby. I missed you," Angie replied warmly, stepping forward to wrap her arms around his neck. "Give me a kiss."

Their embrace was brief but tender.

"I went to the lake. Needed some fresh air. Feeling kind of cooped up in here."

"I know," Angie murmured sympathetically, reaching into the refrigerator to retrieve their beers.

"Tell me about your day?" Henry prompted, as he settled into a chair at the kitchen table.

Angie was already in her bathrobe and her hair was still wet. When he sat, she lifted her leg and placed it in between his, which he in turn rubbed and half-listened as she rambled on about the store owner and customers. This went on for several minutes.

"Are you even listening?" Angie's voice cut through the air in mild frustration.

"What? Yes. I am," Henry replied, tearing his gaze away from the window to focus on her.

She cleared her throat. "Did something happen today? You don't seem yourself," she remarked, taking a slow sip of her drink.

"I, uh, no. I'm fine. Just tired from all the walking I guess."

"Hmmmmm."

Later on, when the two went to bed, he lay on his back as he normally would while his girlfriend dozed in his arms. Usually, he would fall asleep about thirty minutes or so afterward, but not that night. He even tried to close his eyes, but the light from outside was too bright. Instead of attempting to fall asleep, he just lounged there until Angie was in a deep enough sleep that he could move. He eventually did, carefully sliding his arm from underneath her head so that it fell ever-so-gently on her pillow. He shifted to the window, pulling the curtain to one side to view a half-moon that hovered high in the clear sky. He let it close quickly in fear of waking Angie.

It was odd for him to be wide awake at such an early hour and he had no desire to fall back asleep; so off he went, taking careful strides across the creaking wooden planks before finally making it to the stairway. He was careful not to make a sound until he was on the first floor.

"I could use a little help," Henry muttered to himself, his voice echoing softly in the dimly lit kitchen as he rummaged through the cluttered cupboard. He was in search of the bottle of Wild Turkey that he'd spied a few days earlier. It was neatly tucked behind a couple of boxes of cookies; he poured three inches into a glass and tucked the bottle back. He took the cool glass, slipped on a light jacket to ward off the evening chill, grabbed his sneakers, and headed out to stroll along the road. The moon shone down on him like a large spotlight. He stopped for a moment and took in the fresh night air.

"Why did you bring me out here tonight?" he asked while peering up at the moon.

Then he felt it! The moon's pull. The weight of his body shifted forward, causing him to lift one foot off the dirt road, followed by the other, until he found himself in full stride towards it. He took little sips along the way, feeling the liquid burn as it ran into his empty belly.

The moon lit up the road as if there were a dozen streetlights strung along it. As he took long deep breaths, filling his lungs, a smile formed—but he didn't know exactly why. *Maybe it's the air or maybe it's the strange freedom of gallivanting along the dirt road at night without a worry in the world. That's it! My worries had disappeared!*

Any anxiety he had earlier in the day had vanished, and noticing this, he came to a stop, about halfway between Taunton Road and Angie's house. He turned back to view the rooftop.

As he decided his next move, he lifted his whiskey glass high into the sky, the translucent amber liquid catching the moonlight. With a contemplative sigh, he observed the dwindling whiskey remaining in the glass.

"I need more," he muttered to himself, the words carried away on the night breeze as he took the final gulp of whiskey. Turning on his heel, he marched back up the incline, his footsteps echoing in the quiet night air.

Once inside, he placed the glass on the counter and ascended up the stairs, and quietly slipped into bed beside his girlfriend; the warmth of her body a welcome comfort against the chill of the night.

"You're cold, baby," she murmured sleepily, her voice barely audible.

"Shhhhh," he whispered, his arm wrapping protectively around her as they settled into the embrace of sleep.

* * *

Wakey, Wakey!

I left a can of soup out for you. You might like it! It's going to be a rainy day today, so I left some books on the dining room table. Most of these are my dad's.

Have a great day today. Stay warm. See you tonight!

Love,

Angie

With his head still a little tender from the previous night's indulgence, he sipped his coffee and shuffled through the books; it was then he came across *A Farewell to Arms*. He sat on the couch and read the entire morning and afternoon while listening to the rain as it splashed on the windowsill.

1:05 am

(Somewhere between Sudbury Junction and Sioux Lookout)

"That was my first time reading Hemingway's *A Farewell to Arms*," Henry confessed, his voice soft as he turned away to peer out into the enveloping darkness. A weighty silence hung in the air. "Something happened to me when I read that book," he continued, vulnerably. "It completely changed my outlook on life."

He turned to face Thomas, "It basically told me that I hadn't even begun to live life yet," Henry confided. "I was in my mid-twenties and I had never left Canada. Sure, I traveled between Toronto and Victoria, but I hadn't experienced different cultures, different languages, or even different food. I didn't know what it was like to have the living shit scared out of me like men did during wartime." He paused and his gaze drifted downwards to his fidgeting hands. "I felt like a mama's boy. I wasn't a man yet. That's how I felt. There was so much I still needed to do."

Thomas sat in silence, observing Henry's nervous movements with empathy and intrigue, captivated by the raw honesty of his reflection. In the dim light of the train car, Henry still seemed to be reflecting upon his own story.

"Did you say she lived in Whitby?" Thomas asked, leaning forward. "Is that where you're from? I'm the next town over—Ajax."

“I'm from the city. She was from Whitby though.”

"Oh. OK." Thomas fell silent for a moment, his gaze drifting to the window as if lost in thought. "Is that . . . is that the story?"

Henry shook his head. "No, there's more." He glanced at his watch, "It's five after. Let's get some shut-eye. I'll continue this tomorrow if you want to hear the rest."

"Yeah. For sure." Thomas nodded eagerly, settling back into his seat and pulling his jacket closer to use it as a pillow.

Chapter 3 (Thomas)

I closed my eyes, shutting out the world until the man's stirring faded into silence. When I finally dared to open them again, I caught sight of him sprawled on his side like a little boy. I could imagine him resting his head on his mother's lap, consoling him of his hardships. I envisioned her lovingly peering down at him, placing her hand on his head just as she might have when he was a seven-year-old and found out his friend didn't like him anymore. I continued to study the man sleeping as if his mother took on his burden for the night.

Saturday, August 15, 1981 -- 8:15 am EST

I woke to the morning sun blazing through the window and the smell of stale coffee. The aroma was very close, as if it were beside my head. I wasn't sure when I had fallen asleep the night prior and my eyesight was blurry.

"Good morning!" chirped the man across from me. "I brought you a coffee and a croissant."

"Oh," I grumbled, still half-asleep.

I sat up and rubbed my eyes. I didn't feel well-rested and my neck was sore. I was sure my eyebags were clear as day to anyone who looked at me.

"How did you sleep?" the man inquired, his voice breaking the silence of the morning.

"Okay, I guess," I responded, my voice thick with sleep. He reached for the Styrofoam cup wedged between his shoes, extending it toward me with a gesture of kindness. "Here," he offered, a small smile playing at the corners of his lips. "I hope you like cream and sugar."

"Thanks," I said gratefully, taking a sip from the offered cup. He then passed me the pastry, and I accepted it with a nod. Surprisingly hungry, I devoured it in less than a minute, washing it down with another gulp of coffee before letting out a satisfied sigh.

“How did *you* sleep?” I asked.

"So-so, but I’m used to shitty sleep," he replied with a shrug.

We sat in quietness, the acknowledgment of the early morning hanging in the air as we waited for the caffeine to kick in. Finally, I broke the silence.

"Okay," I said, catching Henry's attention as he turned to face me. "So... you were going to continue about Angie."

His eyes lit up with a mischievous grin. "You really want to hear this? I’m not boring you with this stuff, am I?"

"Yes. I mean, no, you're not boring me. Yes, I want to hear it." I chuckled under my breath, "I guess I'm still half-asleep. This train ride is boring."

Chapter 4 (Henry)

The Story of Angie Peterson - Part 2

It was the end of October and Angie came home a little later than she typically did. The aroma of stew Henry was warming wafted from the stove and at the table lay four slices of bread and a generous spread of butter ready for when she finally came home.

"Hi, baby!" Angie exclaimed, shedding her jacket and tossing it onto the sofa with a carefree gesture. "Mmmmm. That stew smells even better than when I first made it!" She crossed the room with a smile, giving her boyfriend a kiss, before sitting at the kitchen table.

He opened the refrigerator, grabbed their beers, and placed them on the kitchen table. He opened the top drawer beside the stove to fetch the bottle opener when his girlfriend cleared her throat rather loudly. He turned and asked, "Is anything wrong?" Henry's concern rippled through his words.

"No. Not quite." Angie's lips twitched with a grin, unable to fully conceal her excitement.

Henry watched her carefully, "What's going on?"

"Sit down. I have some news for you," Angie urged

"Uh oh!"

"It's nothing bad. Well . . . *I* don't think so."

"What's going on?"

Angie took a deep breath and cleared her throat in a nervous gesture before she spoke, "I'm pregnant."

Henry didn't answer.

Angie buried her chin in her chest before blurting, "Henry?"

"I . . . I just . . . wasn't expecting this. Are you sure you're pregnant?" Henry's voice quivered.

"Yes, silly. I wouldn't just spring that on you if I wasn't sure. I saw the doctor today."

"Okay. Wow! Uhm..." He rubbed his hands together, then ran them through his hair. "We're going to have a baby!" Henry's exclaimed words tumbled out in a rush as he leaned back.

"You had me scared for a minute." She heaved out a nervous laugh.

"Sorry. I was in shock. I still am."

"So, make that one beer . . ." Angie nudged her bottle toward him.

"This calls for a drink . . . for me!" Henry exclaimed as he rose from his seat.

He placed the other bottle back in the refrigerator and leaned against the kitchen counter. The two chatted for some time about what was next, but the young man was too distracted to focus on the conversation. He would smile and nod when anything that involved the child came up. The second beer soon followed.

* * *

As the week had gone on, Angie had found herself increasingly exhausted from the long hours at work. One evening, as they sat together listening to the radio, Angie had found herself so weary the music had lulled her off on the couch. It took Henry gently nudging her awake to rouse her from her slumber so they could get themselves ready for bed.

Once under the covers, the two lay beside each other like they normally would. But Henry didn't feel all that tired. So, he meticulously slid out of bed, tip-toed around to the window, and pulled the curtain open to view a full moon, seemingly positioned directly above the house. As he stood, taking in the moon's brilliance, he closed his eyes, basking in its rays, much like one would on a hot summer's day. He enjoyed the moment with no desire to sleep. Instead, he grabbed his clothes, got dressed and quietly made his way downstairs.

Once outside, he made his way around the cedar trees to the middle of the dirt road, where he witnessed the familiar celestial body hovering high in the southern sky. That's when he felt it again - the moon's magnetism pulling him. The pull was even stronger that night! He couldn't understand why.

He continued down the hill towards the moon. There was nothing but silence and the calm breeze moving the dead leaves around the ditch. There was something about being free while out in the middle of the night. It was an intoxicating feeling. He was alive! He could feel it palpitating within him. Something he hadn't experienced since that mid-

September night, sipping that glass of bourbon. Each footstep felt lighter—as if he were walking on pillows.

He continued his leisure walk until he finally reached the bus stop. That's when a gnawing jolt of anxiety hit the pit of his stomach.

He didn't do it right away, but he finally mustered the courage to turn back, casting one last glance at Angie Peterson's home.

He sucked in a large breath, turned back around, and made his way westward along Taunton Road.

* * *

The moon was Henry's friend that night as he walked for hours and hours. It was the fictitious approval he needed because he was certain that he was doing the right thing; that was, of course, until morning broke the night. As the moon faded into the blue sky, his anxiety increased and the knots in his stomach became prominent. His feet were becoming sore from the walk and his legs became heavy and weak. The high that he experienced earlier had now completely vanished. Before entering the bus station, he turned east, squinting from the early morning sun's rays.

"I'm so sorry, Angie."

Once inside the station, he paid and boarded a bus that took him to Toronto, Union Station. Once there he was committed. The next train would be to Vancouver.

Chapter 5 (Thomas)

Saturday, August 15 -- 1981 5:00 pm EST

Henry's voice trembled as he spoke, "You see," he began, his tone heavy with emotion, "This is not the first time I've had to board a train to Vancouver in desperation. No, sir. That time, I ended up moving in with my mother." He turned to stare out the window, the passing landscape a blur. "I never forgave myself for that," he confessed, his voice barely above a whisper. "That was one of the biggest regrets of my life. I never should have left her. I didn't realize it at the time, but..." His eyes met mine, filled with sorrow. "...I loved her."

I was immediately tuned into his use of the phrase "in desperation." *What happened this time? Was it something to do with the man with the beard?*

He continued, "Not only did I leave without an explanation, I left her with a child." His voice broke. He crossed his arms tightly as if to stop himself from crying.

Even though his eyes watered, he was able to refrain from an expulsion of tears. He sighed and held his arms even tighter, turning to view the rugged northern Ontario landscape, his eyes shifting back and forth.

His voice strained, "I never told my mother what I did. She has no idea that I left a young pregnant woman on her own. This... this caring, beautiful and kind woman took me in for two months and I left her with the responsibility of a lifetime." His lips began to quiver. “I'm now forty-five years old and I still remember it so clearly after twenty years."

Henry searched my eyes for judgment. "You must think poorly of me."

My own voice cracked as I responded. "No," I reassured him. "Not at all."

“Oh. You’re just being polite.” His voice cracked and he turned toward the window again.

The afternoon sun was hovering over the western sky as the train rocked back and forth. It was dinner time and I was getting hungry. I peered up at the rocky landscape dotted with tall spruce trees, then turned back to view the man who was also peering out at the scenery while he rubbed his hands together. I could see the pain in his eyes as he gazed ahead. Even though I truly couldn’t empathize with him, I could imagine his pain. It was at this moment that things changed for me. I became curious and sympathetic toward Henry. Oddly enough, I wanted to know other details about this man.

The train came to a stop. We had arrived at Sioux Lookout.

6:30 pm CST (Sioux Lookout)

Henry was very quiet. It seemed like he was a man who always had mental gears turning, but that day it wasn’t just thinking and processing; it was worry and anxiety – that's what I thought. I wished I could just stick a tube in his ear that was somehow connected to his overworked brain, to let all his worries just drain away, like water flowing from a clogged sink.

Darkness eventually took over the orange and pink sky. I twisted back around to stare out of the south facing windows of the train to see a full moon hovering above the eastern landscape. I picked up my book, but every time I began to read, I got this strange sensation that the man across from me was staring at me. I continued looking at paragraph after paragraph, without taking in anything—I was so distracted by the man across from me that I dropped the book quickly to discover that he *was* observing me.

"Are you enjoying it?"

"Yeah. I like Hemmingway. He has a distinct writing style."

The man turned away as if he was already uninterested in continuing the very brief conversation, so I picked up my book once more.

As I went back to my book, he suddenly spoke again. "It's a full moon," he observed.

I dropped the book.

"Yeah. It's really bright tonight," I responded, intrigued by his sudden interest in the moon.

"You know," he continued after a pause, "I can't sleep during a full moon anymore."

"Oh? Why not?"

"One reason is because of what happened with Angie, but not just that," he explained, his voice tinged with unease. "You see, something else happened. It took place when I was a boy. You probably can't relate. I'm sure your father was around when you were a kid." Henry dismissed casually.

"No, not really. Mine died when I was like three." I reflected on the moment my mother told me I had no father. I remember I was about ten when it happened. She said not to worry about it and that many other boys didn't know their fathers either. She never brought it up again and neither did I. My curiosity always burned inside of me, though. Because of this, I was interested in Henry's story of the absence of his father. "So, there's no memory of him, whatsoever," I concluded.

"I see." He nodded.

Chapter 6 (Henry)

Young Henry (1945)

Henry's father's name was Sydney. He was born in the quaint town of Bowmanville, Ontario. Sydney's mother, a woman of English descent, embarked on a journey across the Atlantic to reach Canada alongside her sister in the autumn of 1910. However, fate had a cruel twist in store. Sydney's father, who was supposed to unite with them shortly after was untimely killed in a tragic boiler explosion. Despite this loss, Sydney's mother persevered and raised him on her own. Years passed and she eventually found love again, and Henry's father grew up with three stepbrothers.

Sydney's younger years were shadowed by the tumult of world events, with World War I erupting when he was just a boy. As World War II commenced, he was too old to serve, however he found himself as a worker in a munitions factory. He played a pivotal role in supplying the tools of war to those on the front lines.

On occasions when young Henry wasn't tired, he would wait for his father to return home from work at the factory. His bedroom was on the second floor. It had a dormer window with a ledge large enough to hold Henry's tiny frame. As he sat there he would peer out, like a lookout, and wait until his father strolled home at the end of his shift. Sydney would appear exactly at 11:15 every night. He'd show up at the end of the street with the moonlight creating just enough illumination for the boy to study his father's slow steps toward his house, his metal lunch box swinging in his grasp. He could see how tired his father was.

One evening, during a full moon, he waited by the window for his old man to come home. He remembered distinctly that there was a full moon, because it lit up the hallway leading to his room, casting a long bright moonbeam underneath his bedroom door. Henry's only pet, a black cat named Max, would pace the hallway, casting shadows that stretched into his room. At first, the boy found it creepy until he realized it was just the family pet. Henry recalled that evening opening the door to let Max in. The cat was in a very affectionate mood that night. He purred and rubbed up against his leg seeking attention.

Henry recalled that night specifically because Sydney never came home. The young boy waited for hours until he decided to bring the absence to his mother's attention. He knew something was very wrong when he approached her bedroom, but stopped upon hearing her soft cries from the other side of the cracked wooden door. He returned to his room, sinking onto the window ledge with Max nestled on his lap, finding solace in the quiet companionship until the first light of dawn painted the sky.

Almost every night for two months, Henry sat at the window, waiting for his father. He would wait and wait and see men come home to their families at 11:15 every night. But never a man coming to his family. Another memorable evening that stood out in his mind was when he observed a large gathering of adults, dancing and drinking right in the middle of the street. The young boy later discovered that the neighborhood celebrated the end of the war. The munitions factory closed shortly after, but the boy still waited many nights by the window. He was afraid that if he didn't, his father would never come home. It was almost as if he didn't wait that *one* night, he would jinx any opportunity of his father's final return.

After six months or so, his mother put the house up for sale and they moved to Victoria to live with her sister Gloria. Once they moved in with his aunt, he knew then that he would never see his father again. For years, silent anger brewed within Henry towards his mother, holding her responsible for Sydney's eventual return to a house they no longer called home.

"You know something?" Henry scanned the ceiling of the train car as he thought to himself. "I remember my father saying something to me when I was young. He said, 'There is so much I need to tell you, boy, but not now. When you get older.' I never really knew what he meant by that, but it stuck with me for all those years. I wish I got to hear what he wanted to tell me."

Henry sighed to himself in sadness, then turned to Thomas.

"Anyway. That's why I have trouble sleeping during a full moon," Henry paused. "My father disappeared the night of a full moon. I left my girlfriend, who was with child on a full moon." He continued, studying the young man across from him, expecting a reaction.

Chapter 7 (Thomas)

Sunday, August 16, 1981 -- 1:00 am CST - Winnipeg

The train slowed as it rocked back and forth on the tracks; the echo of the screeching wheels bounced against the neighboring buildings as we pulled into the station. Henry scanned his watch.

"Boy. Time flies." His brow shot up. "It's already one in the morning." He peeked out into the darkness from the window.

Once the train came to a stop, the doors opened and I could feel a cool breeze fill the train car.

"I'm going to get some fresh air," he mentioned as he got up from his seat.

I peered out the window as the overhead lights cast a shadow of his body on the concrete as Henry strolled onto the platform. I continued to study him as he stretched his arms high up into the air and then bent forward to stretch his back. He said something to one of the employees pushing a cart of supplies along the platform. The employee stopped for a moment, answered the inquiry, and then carried on. A gust of wind pushed Henry's hair to one side, which was when he turned to re-enter the train. The rush of wind followed him into the open train car.

"It's beautiful out there. You should get out for some fresh air. It's so . . . stale in here," he snarled as he plopped in his seat. "By the way. We're in Winnipeg."

"I think I'm going to try and get some rest," I replied groggily, curling my jacket together and stuffing it under my neck. "I'm really tired." My mouth opened in an 'O' shape and I let out a huff of air in a breathless yawn.

"Yeah. I think I'll do the same." The man, similar to me, took off his jacket to form a pillow for his head.

"Good night."

"Sweet dreams, my friend," he said as he situated himself in a fetal position on the row of seats across from me. I did the same but had my head towards the windows and my feet facing the aisleway. I had to cover my head with my jacket because the lights of the station scorched through the train car windows. I lay still for a few minutes until I drifted off into a dreamless sleep.

3:00 am CST

In the middle of the night, the train haphazardly jerked forward as it departed the station. I removed my jacket from my head to see the man across from me still sleeping. The jolt of the train didn't seem to wake him. I sat up, stretching out my back and rubbing my eyes. The moon was positioned directly above the train, and its luminance lit up the vast plains of the prairies so clearly that I could almost make out the detail of the landscape.

I was still exhausted, so I lay listening to the train run along the tracks, which I found relaxing. When I closed my eyes to try to think about what beautiful and unworldly things I would see when I arrived in Vancouver, I considered what it would be like to travel to Europe and visit Italy like Hemmingway did. But that quickly faded, as the stories of Henry took over and my sleepy imagination changed to regret and pain. When I reopened my eyes once more, my travel companion remained still, like a little boy. The guilt and hurt I had seen in his face earlier had all but gone. His face held no emotion. It was as if he was oblivious as to what had happened in his conscious state. The man seemed to be at peace; at least while he lie asleep.

As Henry took little breaths in and out, I observed his rubbery face as it jiggled while the train jostled along its tracks. As I continued to study him, I couldn't help but imagine him as the older brother I never had; the one that would make all the mistakes I shouldn't make in life—it was strangely comforting.

Exhaustion was getting the better of me as I struggled to keep my eyelids open. My eyeballs were getting dry and stung each time I tried to watch, so off to sleep I went.

8:05 am

(Somewhere between Winnipeg and Saskatoon)

I woke again to the familiar aroma of coffee, and the golden rays of the morning sun, which seemed to pierce through my eyelids, intensified my weariness. With a groan, I rubbed them for comfort.

"Top of the mornin' to ya!" The man across from me exclaimed.

"Good morning," I replied with a very groggy and tired voice. "What time is it?" I groaned again.

The man checked his watch, "A little after eight." He passed me a coffee and a muffin.

"Thanks."

The bright sun felt strong as it rose high in the sky. For miles and miles, all I could see were fields and fields of wheat. It was calming, watching the stalks blow back and forth in the breeze as the train sped by.

After I finished my muffin, I sensed the man across from me wanted some time alone, so I took out my book by Hemmingway and delved back into the world of Frederic Henry and his escapades in Italy. I read for a good hour or so until I noticed the man across from me becoming increasingly fidgety. I couldn't help but look up. He stretched out his two hands with his palms pressed down on his lap. He studied them carefully looking back and forth at each. I turned to my book but was interrupted.

"What part are you at?" he asked, leaning slightly forward.

"Frederic escapes the police and jumps aboard a train to Milan," I replied, noticing a faint nod of approval from him.

"It's a great book," he said, lost in thought.

I waited for a few minutes, looking out into the abyss of the window, before opening the novel once more. He was still anxious. From the corner of my eye, I noticed that he constantly shifted himself in his seat, letting out grunts and sighs as he did.

"Jesus!" he exclaimed, adjusting awkwardly in his seat again. "These seats get uncomfortable after a while. My ass is numb!"

I chuckled at his remark, feeling the same discomfort.

"I need a shave," he muttered, running his fingers over his two-day stubble. His beard was coming in white, adding a touch of ruggedness to his appearance.

He hunched over suddenly, pulling his suitcase from under his seat, unlatching it before frantically searching.

"Shit!" he cursed, looking up at the ceiling of the car in despair. "I forgot my razor. I was in such a hurry I forgot it." He let out a long huff in disapproval. "Oh well, I guess I'll get another when I get to Victoria." He relatched it in frustration, and shoved it back under his seat.

Once he settled back into his seat, Henry's expression shifted into one I had come to recognize—an uneasy mix of contemplation and regret. It was clear he had more he wanted to confide in me.

"What is it?" I asked.

"I'm such a fuck-up."

"Why do you say that?" I asked with a chuckle in my voice.

“Urgh,” he waved dismissively and turned his head away. “You don’t want to hear another one of my stupid stories, do you?”

“Sure. Why not!”

He snickered at my immediate enthusiasm, but it disappeared just as quickly before he leaned in. “Remember when I asked you to search the car for that bearded man?”

“Yeah. The husky guy you wanted me to look for.” I thought back to that day; it felt like so long ago when I didn't even know Henry's name, anything about Angie, or anything about his life.

“Well, he was following me." His brow rose as he thought. "At least, I thought he was.”

“Following you?”

Chapter 8 (Henry)

"Her name was Cindy. I met her last month; a scorching hot day it was. We crossed paths at this patio joint. Oh, yeah. She was a beautiful blonde, just my type," he recounted, noticing Thomas absorbing every detail. "Do you like blondes?"

"Sure," Thomas answered, not really thinking about the question.

"Me too. Cindy was something else. Instant attraction, you know? We had a two-month love affair and then... then . . . well.." He paused for effect. "Have you ever been in lust?"

"In what?"

"In lust. Not in love, but in lust."

"I don't think so."

"You'd know if you had," he replied confidently.

Henry thought to himself about the love affair he got himself entangled in. He questioned if it had meant as much to her as it did to him. The idea unsettled him, causing him to shift in his seat. Even though the details were still fresh in his head, he paused to reflect on it all before offering a condensed version.

The Story of Cindy

It was July 1st. Henry was tired from strolling Queen Street in the east end of Toronto all morning and afternoon - the sun beaming down on him. While he contemplated the need to find some shade on a patio, he maneuvered through the crowds on the sidewalk, which were full of sun-seekers walking to and from the lake. He passed a long lineup of patrons waiting to put their ice cream order in at a nearby parlor, taking in the sweet smell of the waffle cone press as he passed.

He continued his way up Queen Street until he reached a patio on the corner of Queen and Beech Avenue called The Catamaran.

"For two?" the host asked.

"Just one."

The host placed the menu on the table, which was situated beside a metal railing, with servers scurrying back and forth on the other side. The table was still wet from the last customer. He studied the menu but was more interested in having a cold beer than eating. Before he placed the menu down, he peered over the top of it to catch a blonde woman sitting across from him. She gazed at him long enough for him to notice, then slowly turned back to her friend and smiled. The blonde woman's hair cascaded in loose waves around her shoulders, and her eyes were mesmerizing and sparkled in the bright sunlight. She wore a figure-hugging dress in a bright shade of white. Her makeup was fresh and her rosy lip color added to her undeniable charm. She was elegant and sultry. Her friend had shoulder-length brown hair and wore sunglasses. *She* also made no effort to hide the fact that she was gawking. She turned back to her blonde friend and leaned in to express a comment that was followed by a giggle.

It had been a while since Henry received attention from an attractive woman. He tried to remain composed, but when he placed his arm on the table to pull his chair in, he felt a slimy substance on his elbow. He turned his arm to reveal a blotch of mustard. He sheepishly searched for a napkin.

"Why don't you sit over here? It's been cleaned," said the brunette with sunglasses, pointing to the table beside them.

"Thank you. I think I will." He stood in confidence. The blonde beamed at her friend with astonishment.

"Here," the woman with the sunglasses said, holding out a fresh napkin.

"Thanks."

Henry sat at the tiny table, which was positioned so that he was directly facing the blonde. Her brunette friend adjusted her chair slightly so that she could face him too.

"So . . . is your wife out shopping or something?" The brunette leaned forward slightly, her glossy lips leaving a faint mark on the rim of her glass as she took a sip of her drink. She tapped her foot against the ground as she awaited a response.

"Ahhh . . . No," he answered, a little surprised by the woman's directness. "No wife. Just me."

The server approached: "Are you ready to order?"

"A pint of draft, please," Henry requested.

The server nodded, "Anything from the menu?"

"No, thanks. Just the beer for now."

"Certainly," she replied with one eyebrow slightly raised, turned, and darted toward the server entrance.

"Excuse me," Henry called to gain her attention, then turned to the two women. "How are your drinks?"

"Oh! I'll take another Margarita please," the brunette chimed in eagerly.

Turning to the blonde woman, Henry offered a friendly yet nervous inquiry. "And for you?"

"I'm good," the blonde replied with a casual wave of her hand. "Thanks for asking."

"So," the server asked, "is this on your bill or . . ." Her pen bopping between Henry and his new guests.

"On mine, please," he replied, then turned to the two women. "I'm Henry by the way,"

“Nice to meet you,” the woman with the sunglasses said. “I’m Nancy, and this is Cindy.” She gestured towards her blonde friend.

“Nice to meet you.” After a brief pause, Henry's gaze shifted to Cindy, studying her for a moment before offering a nod of acknowledgment.

Nancy adjusted herself in her chair before speaking up, "I have to admit, we noticed when you first came in. You remind us of someone we used to know." She glanced at her friend and added, "Don't you think?"

Cindy’s eyes enlarged, once again stupefied by her friend’s comment. She didn’t reply and instead pursed her lips.

"Oh?" He inquired. "What was he like?" Nancy turned to her friend briefly then back to him with a snicker.

"Let's leave that topic for now. So, tell me. What's a man like you doing all alone on a beautiful sunny day like this? I mean, are you meeting someone. . . were you shopping? It's a holiday after all."

The server brought their drinks.

"Just . . . having a pint to myself," Henry responded, then scanned the blonde woman who hadn't said much up to that point, although she had been listening with some intensity. "You seem awfully quiet."

Cindy had hazel eyes and a very prominent jawline, which was beautifully sculpted. She seemed to be the kind of woman who held herself well poised, regardless of any emotion she retained internally. When she positioned herself upright, her back arched in such a way, pushing her breasts forward, striking a sexual vibe in Henry.

"I've been listening," Cindy responded. "You sound quite intelligent. You're nothing like the man that you reminded us of earlier." She lifted her wine glass to her lips.

"Thank goodness for that . . . I think!" he sounded befuddled. "Cheers." He took a sip of his beer and broke away to study the beads of condensation that ran down his glass. That's when he noticed, from the corner of his eye, the blonde studying him. In turn, her friend studied her. Henry raised his head so that his eyes met the woman he had been admiring.

“Look who’s blushing! Something on your mind?” Nancy asked him as happy lines formed around her mouth.

He chucked, but lacked much of a reply. Instead, he began with, “OK. My turn for questions. Are *you* taking a break from shopping? Are *your* husbands not going to join you on the patio later?”

Cindy straightened herself; her back no longer curved, to Henry’s dismay. She casually rubbed her left hand with her right, concealing her ring finger.

"My husband is at home cutting the lawn," Nancy replied, then turned to her friend. "But this one isn't married anymore."

Cindy shot Nancy a sharp look.

"Does she always speak for you?" Henry guided his question towards Cindy.

"She's taken the liberty today," Cindy half-snapped at Nancy, her lips pursed.

"Oh, stop it. Big deal. There's lots of divorced women out there. Now you two have something in common. He's single, you're divorced." Nancy said, waving her forefinger between the two.

Cindy sat quietly, eventually releasing her right hand. There was no ring, but an indentation of where one once was.

"Excuse me, please." Cindy pushed her chair out from under her causing a loud scrape against the patio stone. "I need to visit the ladies' room."

Henry bit his bottom lip but didn't follow the *click-clack* of her heels.

"Oh, wow!" Nancy exclaimed. "She's in a mood! I try to do something simple . . ." She shook her head, removed her sunglasses, and rubbed the area just below her eyes. "She's got a thing for you. She just doesn't know how to handle herself around an attractive man." Nancy placed her sunglasses on the table. "You *are* single . . . right?"

"Yes. Why do you ask?"

"Cindy is a long-time friend. She doesn't need any more bullshit in her life." The woman paused and studied his face for a moment. "You seem like a decent guy."

Nancy was also about the same age as her blonde friend, but less gentle. Her right arm hung on the back of her chair before continuing, "You should join us for dinner later. But I can't ask you in front of her," she said, still focused on her thoughts. "Tell you what, when she comes back, go to the men's room or make a call or something. Okay?"

"All right." He continued studying the beads of sweat the humidity created on his glass. From his peripheral, the familiar blonde hair bopped up and down as Cindy strode towards them. He made every attempt not to look up as she arrived, but couldn't help himself, lifting his head to admire the sight of her newly applied lipstick and freshly brushed hair.

"Oh!" Henry exclaimed. "I just remembered, I need to place a call." He checked his watch. "I'll be right back."

He made his fake phone call, stood in the phone booth which was just inside the entrance of the restaurant, waited a minute or two, then returned. Once he took his seat, he felt a hint of tension coming from the two women across from him. They sat silent until Nancy stood abruptly and stomped past Henry's table.

"Excuse me."

The man sat at the table, not knowing what to say, took his index finger and ran it up and down his beer glass, rubbing away the last of the beads.

"Henry!" Cindy called.

He turned to face her.

"I think my friend is up to some kind of crazy idea about asking you to join us for dinner." She raised her chin before continuing. "First of all, she's married!" she said with her face tightening. "Secondly, I'm recently divorced. I'm the furthest . . ." The volume of her voice was gradually rising but she stopped and leaned in slightly before continuing with a low voice. "Secondly. I'm the furthest from being ready to meet someone." She paused. "I'm sorry about all this drama. I love my friends, but I wish they'd . . ."

He shifted himself upright in his chair.

"It's OK," he replied, nodding his head. "Hey. We just met. Let's just . . . enjoy cold drinks on a patio. You can't beat that on a nice day like this!" he said, gulping his beer.

The pause in conversation was awkward for the middle-aged man to the point he found it difficult to make eye contact. She repositioned herself in such a fashion that her right leg crossed over her left with the tip of her shoe pointed towards him, almost purposefully. While she studied the man, she slid her thumb and finger up and down the stem of her now empty wine glass. Her body language became relaxed, which contradicted her earlier mood. He adjusted himself in his chair.

"Give me your number!" she said rather sternly. "I'll call you." She reached into her purse. "God! I need a smoke! I hope you don't mind." She pulled out a pack of Du Maurier cigarettes.

"Not at all."

She lit her cigarette and ripped the top off its box, handing it to him, along with a pen.

"Here."

He wrote down his number and passed it back, which she quickly stuffed into her purse.

She exhaled and continued to study the man. "My… My…" She muttered, shaking her head before letting out a sigh.

"How about another glass?" he offered while raising his beer.

"Sure. I could use one more before dinner."

Nancy interjected with a grin as she settled into her seat, "Well, boys and girls? What's the plan for this evening?" the sunlight catching the subtle highlights in her chestnut hair, accentuating her animated expression.

"Henry is going to join us for another drink," Cindy prompted firmly, following the movement of her friend. "But he won't be staying for dinner."

"Oh." Her disappointment was potent. "That's a shame."

* * *

It was another scorching day in July when Henry was sprawled out on the couch. Several fans hummed in the background, trying to cool him off but they failed to provide much relief. Right before he cracked open a novel, the shrill ring of his phone echoed throughout the room.

“Hello.”

“Hi. Is this Henry?”

“Yes, speaking.”

“It’s Cindy, from the patio.”

“Hi. Yes. I remember you.” Henry grinned to himself.

“I’m sorry it took so long to get back to you.” He listened to her take a puff from her cigarette, and then exhale. “It’s been a hectic.” She paused. “Am I interrupting something?”

"Not at all. I was just about to settle in with a book."

"Oh."

There was a momentary pause, filled with the distant sound of traffic passing by outside Henry's window. He waited as she continued to seemingly enjoy her cigarette.

"Are you free tonight to meet for a drink?" she asked.

"You mean . . . tonight, tonight?"

"Yes. Tonight," she replied without any change in her tone.

"Where did you have in mind?"

"Louie's," she said. "It's a piano bar on Queen West."

"Um… OK." He looked at his watch. "What time did you have in mind?"

"I still need to get ready, but I can make it there for eight," she replied taking another puff of her cigarette. "So . . ." She paused again. "Are we going to meet? Or no? You sound… reluctant"

"No. I mean . . . yes. I want to meet. I'm not reluctant. I was just a little surprised. I'll see you at Louie's at eight."
He fell back in his chair.

"That was the first red flag," Henry recounted in frustration, his gaze fixed on the young man. "Then came the whole 'can you meet tonight' bullshit. God, what a fool I was. Anyway," he concluded, shaking his head slightly as if to shake off the memory.

The Story of Cindy: Part 2

Henry parked his car two blocks away from Louie's and strode towards Queen Street West, his shirt already sticking to him from the humidity that hung in the air. The establishment was dimly lit with a long bar situated to his right and several two-seater tables scattered along the left, one of which Cindy sat at. She was wearing a fitted blue dress that stopped above her knee, revealing her tanned, toned legs. Her luscious blonde hair was pin-straight and glided elegantly down her back. She was resting against the back of her chair, appearing relaxed. As he came closer, the left side of her lips formed a devilish grin.

"Hello," she greeted, her voice perfectly steady. "Right on time, I see. Don't you look nice!" She complimented.

"Thank you. You look as good as the first time we met." His voice shook a bit, but his smile was genuine.

The room was dark except for the soft glow emanating from a small light above the tinkling piano behind him.

"Nice place!" he remarked, his eyes wandering around the room.

"I almost didn't call you," Cindy admitted, her tone matter-of-fact.

"What?" His curiosity piqued; he leaned in slightly. "Why is that?"

"I'm nervous about meeting another man. I changed my mind twice while I was getting dressed."

He pulled his chair closer. "What do you mean?"

"Listen. I'm newly divorced and not looking to have another man in my life anytime soon." She raised her eyebrows provoking a reaction. "While we were at the patio last weekend, I made a silly comment to my girlfriend about you and so she starts . . . well, you know how that played out."

Henry was initially put off by how the conversation was starting. He even considered if he just wasted a perfectly good evening when he could have been home relaxing.

"What would you like to drink, sir?" asked the male server who approached the table, seemingly out of nowhere.

"I'm not ready to order yet. Can you give us a minute please?" Henry fleetingly glanced at the menu.

"Of course," the server responded, with a French accent.

Cindy smirked, her eyes gleaming with mischief. "Going somewhere?"

"So, why exactly did you call me to ask me out for a drink then?" Henry inquired, studying her expression for any hints.

"I don't know," Cindy replied casually, her poker face giving nothing away. "Can we order now?"

Henry settled back into his seat, reaching for the menu again. After a moment, he turned to flag down the server. "Excuse me! We're ready now."

"Madam?" the server inquired, ready to take her order.

"A glass of Pinot Grigio, please," Cindy requested.

"And, sir?" the server turned to Henry.

"Cab Sav," Henry replied.

The server nodded and gracefully glided away.

"You look a little tense," she remarked. "Why don't you relax a little?" she said, rocking her leg that was crossed over her knee.

"So should you." His fingers touch the top of her shin to steady it.

"We're going to get along just fine, I think," she commented, reaching for her purse, searching briefly before holding up a Du Maurier box. "You don't mind, do you?"

"Not at all, no."

She lit her cigarette, letting out her first puff.

"You don't smoke, do you?" Cindy positioned her elbow on the tiny table, smoke forming a tale which circled above her head and up to the ceiling.

"Nope. Never have."

What made you come out tonight, Mr. Henry?" Cindy's voice was playful and curious. "Nothing better to do?"

"Well, ah . . . what?" He finally caught her last comment. "I wanted to see you."

"Oh? So, what is it you wanted to see? What exactly is it about me that you like?" Her fingers tapped lightly on the table as she spoke.

She brought the cigarette to her mouth and took a long drag.

He leaned in, "I'm attracted to you, Cindy. I think you're gorgeous."

Cindy awkwardly blew out her smoke before she could fully inhale it. "Really? Huh! Pretty bold of you to say."

She finally looked away, uncrossed her legs, and then leaned in with her arms folded in front of her. "What is it you want from me? Sex? Is that it?"

"Can a man not express his attraction to a woman without it just being about sex?"

Cindy's eyes were still fixated on her date. "Not really. It eventually comes out at some point."

She sat back and reached for her cigarette, holding it without taking it away from the ashtray.

The server had arrived, but neither of them paid him any mind. "Madam . . . sir," He placed the drinks on their table.

"Thanks!" Cindy flashed a quick smile at the server, her eyes lingering on Henry until the server left. "But that's OK. At least you made it . . . somewhat clear what you want from me."

She lifted her cigarette to her mouth and took another puff, the tendrils of smoke curling around her face. "And I'm OK with that, by the way."

"Cheers to that!"

"Cheers, Mr. Henry!" Their glasses clinked together, the sound echoing in the dimly lit bar.

* * *

The couple spent the next two hours getting acquainted whilst listening to the nostalgic sounds of the piano in the background. The conversation was playful and simple, but certainly not deep. There were unspoken boundaries that Henry avoided, which made the chit-chat easy and relaxed.

"Well," Cindy said as she studied her empty glass. "I think I should head back now."

Henry pulled his wrist out to check the time.

"Excuse me a minute." She stood, and moved gracefully toward the bar, allowing the seated man to enjoy her body movements. He watched as she leaned against the edge of the bar to gain the bartender's attention. She made her request. He quickly nodded, then reached for the phone.

"What was that all about?" Henry asked.

"I ordered a cab."

"I could have given you a lift. Have him cancel it. I'll take you home," he asserted, standing and reaching for his keys.

"No. Sit down. I'll wait. It's already on the way."

Cindy's body language and mood changed once again. He could feel her edginess come back, so he relented and let the weight of his body hit the back of the chair. There was tension between the two that was eventually broken by the French server.

"Madam?" The server's voice cut through their conversation, drawing their attention. "Your cab is waiting." He gestured towards the entrance with a subtle nod, indicating the waiting taxi.

Henry paid and followed his date to the waiting cab, pulling the car door open for her while she flowed into the seat, backside first, followed by her legs, her knees elegantly pressed together.

"You can kiss me good night." She peered up from the open rear door.

He leaned down, still holding the car door. The kiss was long enough for him to taste the sweet remnants of the wine on her lips. The release was beautiful, ending in a delightful smack. Cindy's hands remained on his face for a moment afterward.

"Good night, Henry." The warm tingle he felt afterward lingered, leaving him wanting more.

* * *

The next morning, Henry woke with a rushing sensation as if he had forgotten something of importance. Nothing came to mind except his recollection of the evening before. The images of that night ran through his mind as he lay in bed; the kiss, touching her leg, her smell. The thoughts excited him so much that he felt an urge to rush to the phone and dial her number.

"Dammit! I don't even have her number."

* * *

Cindy called five days later in the afternoon and asked if he would like to meet her again at Louie's that evening.

Louie's was very busy that night. The anxious man struggled to find his date, as there were only small lights on the tables and the room was filled with pungent cigarette smoke.

"There you are!" He exclaimed with a grin as he finally spotted his date, her cheek already angled to receive his kiss. He closed the gap between them with a swift step, planting a gentle peck on her cheek.

She wore tight-fitted jeans, black stiletto heels, and a white blouse.
He was so preoccupied with his immediate attraction that he couldn't form any opening dialogue. Instead, he sat at the table rubbing his hands together thinking of what to say.

"Sir?" asked the French server, breaking the silence.

"I think I'm going to have a beer tonight," Henry confirmed.

"Madame?" He peered down at her half-full wineglass. She waved her hand, gesturing that she was fine, and the server scurried off into the smokey darkness.

Henry turned to the piano, but no one was behind it. However, a tiny light over it was still on.

"No music tonight?"

"Louie will be back."

"Oh. That's Louie? The owner?"

"Yep! You okay, Mr. Henry? You seem preoccupied."

"Why do you call me Mr. Henry?"

"I don't know. It suits you, and I don't know your last name."

"Oh . . . well, it never came up. It's . . . "

"Don't tell me!" Cindy made up a halting motion with her hand.

"Huh?"

"It wouldn't be fair, as I'm not going to tell you mine," she said impassively.

"Really? We're going to play this *Cat and Mouse* game again, are we?" He fell back in his chair, turning away.

"Come on." Cindy leaned forward and slid her hand across the table.

He peered down at it before placing his over top.

"Sir?" the server interrupted.

Henry leaned back, removing his hand so that the waiter could place the beverage in front of her.

"Pardon."

Cindy didn't move her hand, instead, she tapped the table for him to re-engage. He did so and caressed the length of each finger. When he reached her ring finger, she attempted to pull away but Henry held it still, glancing up to view her lips pressed together in disapproval. In an attempt to relax his date, he slid his hand underneath hers, rubbing the palm with his fingertips.

"So, we know each other as Mr. Henry and Cindy, Huh?" Henry finally grinned. "Fair enough."

She squeezed his hand with a reassuring smile. "Be patient with me."

"I'm trying," Henry replied, his tone earnest.

"Madame et Monsieur." Louie approached their table. "Do you 'ave any requests?" He inquired the couple.

Louie was a plump and jolly-looking man with black slicked-back hair and a pencil mustache. His olive skin was tanned and oily. With a notepad held in one hand and a pen in the other, he turned to face Cindy, then Henry, and back to Cindy.

She turned to her date for a suggestion but he shrugged his shoulders.

"Misty. Play Misty," Cindy requested, her voice soft.

"Oui," Louie jotted it down on a small notepad, giving a quick nod before moving on to the next table.

Cindy glanced at Henry with a mischievous glint in her eyes. "Don't you think that's funny?"

"What's that?" Henry replied.

"You know the song, 'Misty'?"

"I think so?"

"You don't know the movie? *Play Misty for Me*, starring Clint Eastwood?" she quizzed.

"Yeah, but I've never seen it. Is it about the song, 'Misty'?"

"It's a thriller. I wanted to hear the song and as soon as I asked, it reminded me of the movie title. Anyway, forget it. You didn't get the joke," she said, searching her purse for a cigarette, before lighting it, then tossing her lighter back in.

With her back pressed against her chair, holding the cigarette beside her, she dropped her chin, adjusted her shoulders, and pushed her chest out before asking: "Do you like what you see?" she asked with a demeanor change, holding his gaze.

"Of course!"

"What is it you like?" She took a puff.

"Your beautiful face."

She exhaled, tilting her head upwards to let the smoke rise. "Oh, come on! You can do better than that!"

Henry chewed on his lip before speaking, "I like your figure."

"Are you new at this or something? Have you never flirted with a woman before? You need to turn up the heat a little, Mister!" Cindy teased, a devilish grin spreading across her face.

Henry paused, unsure how to respond to her playful challenge.

"I wore this top for you. Don't you like it?" Cindy asked, taking another puff from her cigarette.

"I do. I like it a lot, actually."

"Why?" she pressed, her eyes fixed on him expectantly.

He studied the thin fabric of her blouse, specifically the lovely mounds that her bra barely covered. The thought of his hands caressing her aroused him, but he couldn't get the words out in an elegant way.

Cindy leaned in closer, her words carrying a boldness that caught Henry off guard. "I think you should fuck me," she stated bluntly, her eyes fixed on his reaction. "And I don't mean tonight."

Henry blinked in surprise at her straightforwardness.

"I didn't even answer you," he managed to say.

Cindy leaned back in her chair, a sly smile playing at the corners of her lips. "Hmmm. I see. Look who's playing now?"

"I'm not," Henry protested.

"Really? But I want you to," Cindy replied, her gaze steady.

"Okay fine then," Henry relented, leaning in closer. "Let's play."

"That's better." She took one last puff, exhaled, and put out her cigarette. "Tell me. Why haven't you made a comment about my breasts? Most men like them," she remarked.

"I didn't think it was appropriate."

"Really? I already told you, I'm not jumping into another relationship. I thought I made myself clear the other night."

"Yeah. You did."

"OK then. So, what's appropriate now?"

Henry found himself at a loss for words. He was baffled by Cindy's change in behavior as if a switch just flicked on.

"I don't know. You *tell* me." He rested against the back of his chair.

"Hmmm, I think I can do better then *tell*."

She got off her chair and took cat-walk-like strides toward the bar where she spoke with the bartender, and slid him a banknote before continuing to the ladies' room. Henry sat perplexed, as he assumed she had ordered another cab, but he didn't notice the man behind the bar reach for the phone.
After a few minutes, Cindy's sensuous silhouette reappeared from the smoke-filled hallway. He enjoyed the sway of her hips as she moved. It wasn't until she was within a few feet that he discovered the curves of her breasts flowing freely beneath her blouse. *Did she remove her bra?* He thought to himself.

“Come on. Let’s go! I’ve already paid.” She stood in front of him.

“Ah . . . okay.”

She slid her hand around his left arm as they exited the bar. “Where’s your car?”

"Just around the corner."

"So..." Henry hoarsely cleared his throat. "What are we doing?"

"Oh, my God," She sighed, shaking her head with laughter. "Just drive down to the lake, will you?"

Once in the vehicle, Henry hastily navigated through the side streets until he found a small lane close to the water.

"Park here," Cindy instructed as they reached their destination.

He pulled up along the curb of a dead-end, the car now overlooking the serene waters of the lake.

Her eyes darted towards him. “Kiss me,” She whispered as she leaned in.

Henry looked back towards her. He couldn't help himself. He grabbed her by the waist, twisting his body while he remained in the driver's seat.

He wanted to be soft with her, gentle. But she quickly grew impatient. She pulled him closer to her, wanting no space in between their bodies. He slid his hand from her waist up her side, but she intervened, placing it over her exposed breast.

"Please…" She moaned. "Touch me. I want you to feel me." She pleaded to him desperately.

He slowly maneuvered himself on top of her, and she slid down her seat. When he was situated and her seat was pushed back, she slowly dragged her delicate fingers along his thighs. They moved deliberately until they settled on his hardened crotch.

"Oh yeah," she said with a throaty groan. "I can feel you. I like it!"

Henry's head hit the roof liner of the car as she continued to slide her hand along his erection.

"Let's go in the back," he breathily offered.

"No," she said firmly. "Touch me. I want you to touch me." She guided his hand in between her legs, closing her eyes as he obliged. She extended her openness as he continued pressing and gently rubbing, further arousing his date to the point that she clenched her hand on his shirt, scrunching it as she did, catching a bit of his skin in her fingernails.

With her eyes still closed, she let out a long pleasurable breathy, "Oh . . . f u c k . . ."
The rhythm of her breathing slowed and the grip on his shirt eventually loosened. She then raised her hand to her forehead.

"Oh, God." She hurriedly reached between her legs. "I can't believe I came in your car." She covered her mouth, chuckling to herself.

Henry crawled back into his seat and studied her abashed face.

"I'm so embarrassed!" Her hand remained. Her eyes were wide and her chest heaved as she caught her breath.

"You okay?"

"Yeah… I'm fine. I'm just a little…. discombobulated, that's all." She searched for her purse to fish out her bra. "Turn your head. I need to put this back on. Phew!" she exclaimed, stretching her hands behind her back. "Take me back, please."

The car remained silent on the return drive to Louie's. Henry cast quick side glances at his date while she applied a fresh coat of lipstick.

"Well, that was fun!" Henry said as he placed the car into park. His date didn't acknowledge the sarcasm.

She instead grabbed her purse and leaned in for a kiss, "I have to go."

"Why . . ." he started before stepping out of the car, standing behind its open door. "Why don't I give you a lift home?" he asked as she continued towards the bar.

"I'm going to get a cab," she said without looking back. "Thanks, though."

He studied the swing of her hips which was in perfect rhythm to the *click-clack* of her heels. Once underneath the awning of Louie's, she approached the doorman, who leaned in to hear her request. He entered the bar. Cindy remained and lit a cigarette as she waited. Henry returned to his vehicle and waved as he drove by, disturbed by the fact that she didn't return the gesture.

"What the hell is wrong with this woman?" he said aloud to himself.

"Jesus! What the hell?"

He circled the block to drive back to where he had dropped his date, but stopped far enough so that she couldn't see him. She was still waiting, holding her cigarette, watching a streetcar screech by. Her face was completely stoic. Eventually a cab arrived, the doorman opened the car door, and off she went. Henry shifted the car into drive.

Although he hated the idea of tailing her, he needed to know more about the woman. She was a mystery to him. He continued following for almost thirty minutes east on Queen while maintaining a safe distance.

The cab finally turned onto a side street populated with mature trees and luxurious homes along each side. The vehicle drove slowly until it stopped midway up the incline. The light inside switched on exposing her movements. From his vantage point, he studied her as she reached into her purse to pay the driver and let herself out.

She strode up the driveway towards a large stone house. Before he left, he reached into his glove box for a pen, wrote down the house number on the palm of his hand, and then drove to the end of the street to note the street name—Devon Street.

He eventually drove home, opened a beer, sat on his couch, and asked himself:

"Who the hell is this woman?"

* * *

As the days went by, Henry's expectations of seeing Cindy again faded. He even checked the phone for a dial tone, which made him feel so foolish that he just made a point of pushing her out of his mind completely. Part of him wanted nothing more to do with her as he found her sudden mood changes disturbing. But if he had to be completely honest with himself, he couldn't stop thinking about her.

What is it that's driving me wild about this woman? Why am I risking my sanity? Is it her movie-star-like charisma, her elegant and alluring body language, or perhaps it's her enigmatic eyes or seductive smile? What the hell is it?

A week went by and just as he was almost getting through a full day without thinking of Cindy and her captivating ways, the phone rang. When it did, he knew it was her. He couldn't relate it to anything he'd experienced before, but he knew.

"Hello?" Henry asked in anticipation. There was a short pause.

"Hi." A feminine voice rang through the telephone. "Remember me?"

"Yes, Cindy. I know it's you." Henry's voice softened, he paused, deliberating about what to say next before asking, "What have you been up to?"

She exhaled at the question. "Oh. . . this and that, not much."

There was another awkward pause and a silence lingered between them.

As he sat with the phone pressed against his ear, he felt that they were starting all over again, the games, the silence, the second-guessing. It frustrated him, but he was hooked and he knew it. He waited, determined not to make the next comment.

"What are you doing tonight?" she asked.

"I . . ." he hesitated for a moment, considering his response. "I'm . . .

sipping a beer, relaxing. Why? What are you doing?"

"I'm talking to you, silly!" Her playful tone danced through the line.

He let out a soft chuckle, glancing at the time on his watch which read 7:30pm.

"Well, how about joining me for a drink?"

"Seriously?"

"Absolutely."

"Okay," she agreed without hesitation.

With a sudden burst of energy, he rose from his seat.

"Hello?" Cindy's voice brought him back to the moment.

"Yes. I'm here. Give me an hour and I'll be ready," he said, eyeing the clutter in his apartment.

"Address, please."

* * *

An hour passed when finally, a knock at the door. Cindy was dressed in white jeans, black stilettos, and a silky black blouse, presenting a bottle of wine.

"Hi, handsome. I brought this."

"Hello, Cindy." He greeted his guest with a kiss.

Her eyes glanced around, "This is a cozy little place!" She strolled around the couch and toward the large bay window, peering out as she clutched her white purse firmly.

Henry studied her figure but was caught when she promptly turned.

"Have a seat," he said, nervously.

She took a seat comfortably and placed her purse on the floor, crossing one leg over the other, and resting her back against the large wingback chair. Sporting her usual grin, which Henry had become familiar with, she studied him as he brought the two glasses to the seating area. He poured the wine.

"Cheers!"

"Cheers, Mr. Henry."

As they sat, Henry had temporarily forgotten that he followed her home the previous week. He decided to take the opportunity to find out if she would divulge anything.

"So, where exactly do you live? I meant to ask you the other night," Henry inquired. His leg bounced as he waited for her to respond.

Cindy took a thoughtful sip from her drink before replying, "I'm in the west end."

Although he caught her lie, he didn't challenge her.

"Why?" Cindy's gaze lingered on him. "Is it important for you to know where I live?" There was a subtle tension in her voice, her lips tightening slightly. She lowered her chin; her eyes locked with his as she anticipated a further response, her foot bopping as it had on their first date. He reached to steady it, then slid his fingers under her foot.

"No, not really. Just making conversation," he replied, trying to diffuse any tension.

Cindy didn't respond. Her eyes were fixated on him while he caressed her foot, which she enjoyed. His need to know more about her diminished as his physical attraction took over and anything that she was hiding didn't seem to matter anymore.

Cindy tapped her fingers lightly on the couch, her expression turning slightly impatient. "Don't you have any music?" she asked, breaking the silence.

"Yes, I do," he said with a grunt as he lifted himself off the chair. He got up and thumbed through his record collection. "I hope you like jazz. That's pretty much all I got." He slipped the vinyl out of its dust cover and placed the needle into the groove. "That's fine," she said, her foot still bobbing up and down.

He returned, leaned forward, and reached out to steady her foot once again, but this time, held her ankle firmly as he undid the strap of her stiletto. He removed it and waved for the other, which she gracefully presented by switching one leg over the other. Still holding her ankle, he caressed her foot, rubbing the arch, then moving towards the tender spot above her heel. He studied the bridge of her foot, caressing it with his fingertips which caused her to pull away.

"That tickles." She flinched. Yet, didn't release.

"You like watching me squirm?" she asked.

Henry grinned.

She didn't let him continue very long. She stood and positioned herself in front of him. "Where's your bedroom?"

* * *

After they made love, Henry opened his eyes, watching the spinning of the ceiling fan, which blew its rhythmic breeze on their naked bodies. While he soaked in the euphoria, Cindy slid her hand under his arm, pulling her body close to his. He turned on his side so that they could face each other.

Cindy's smile widened. "I think I'm liking you more," she said, her eyes twinkling.

"Oh, really?"

"Yes, Mr. Henry," Cindy said playfully, leaning in closer.

"That's good to hear."

"Kiss me."

He grabbed her waist, pulling her against him. His sheets wrapped around her figure. To Henry, she was a completely different woman than the seductive and enigmatic woman he met at Louie's. She was relaxed. Her eyes had a softness that he hadn't seen before.

"Such a handsome face." She pushed the loose hair away from his forehead.

As he lay there, he knew that he was falling for her. There had been just a few moments in his life where Henry wished time could stand still. That was certainly one of them.

* * *

The two continued to see each other in this fashion: once a week or so, in the evening between eight and midnight, with nothing more than an hour's notice. There was even one day she stayed for the entire afternoon and evening, and it was that particular day that he knew he fell in love with her. They lay in bed, caressing, talking, or sometimes they would just remain silent, not uttering a single word. But like every other time she came over, she had to go home. She would never just sleep over so that they could wake together. This bothered him immensely.

One evening when she visited, she seemed different; she was curt and abrupt. It appeared as if she was on a mission to come to his house, have quick sex and then swiftly depart.

"I need a cigarette," Cindy declared as she hopped off the bed, put on her undergarments and then stormed down the hallway towards the living room.

Henry lay for a moment before getting up, slipping into his boxers and pants. He casually strode back to the living room where his lover held her cigarette high with her right hand, her one leg crossed over the other and bobbing up and down hastily. That was the indicator.

"Grab me an ashtray, will you?" she asked impolitely.

Cindy didn't say anything else but followed him as he placed it on the coffee table before he took his seat.

"What time is it?" she asked, her voice shook with impatience.

"Uhh . . . let me check," he let out a sigh and got up once more to check the time on the stove. "It's 10:30."

"Shit!" She flicked her ashes onto the ashtray and blew out the smoke she had inhaled moments ago. "I'd better get going."

"Really?"

"Yeah, really." She squished the last of her cigarette in the ashtray.

He thought about confronting her, but he knew it wouldn't have ended well. He didn't want to lose what he had, even though it was far from perfect.

She dressed haphazardly and headed straight for the phone to call a cab.

He knew there was a reason for her sudden departure, but he wasn't in the mood to ask, which would have only led to a fight. Once off the couch, he peered outside at the wet streets, before turning, leaning against the window ledge, arms crossed as he waited for his guest to leave.

"Kind of far away, aren't you?" she said after she hung the receiver onto its cradle.

Reluctantly, he paced toward her.

"Good night!"

"'night."

After hovering at the top of the stairs, holding the door open, he closed it and turned the lights off in his apartment before racing towards the window. As Cindy stood waiting for a cab, she lit another cigarette, taking a few puffs until the car eventually pulled up to the curb. She threw the cigarette onto the wet sidewalk, got into the vehicle, and off it went—that was Henry's cue. He grabbed his jacket and scurried down the stairs and out the back way to his car.

He finally caught up with the cab but kept his distance. The rain had stopped, but the roads were still wet. The other vehicle's headlights glimmered as they sped by, the remnants of the day's filth splashed their underbellies. The cab turned right on Devon Street and stopped in the same spot as before, but this time, took off once more before coming to a final stop.

Henry peered through the fogged windshield to see the cabbie turn the light on, but she didn't leave right away. Instead, the driver waited as Cindy brushed her hair before getting out. Once out, her stride was slow and cautious as she approached her house which was, unlike last time, well-lit. Also contrasting was the sight of a black Crown Victoria parked in the driveway. Once in front of it, she stopped to place her palm over the hood, then continued up the pathway and inside. Henry pulled his car closer and reached over to roll down the passenger window to get a better view. He saw Cindy's blonde head pass the front window and then out of sight. A moment later, a bald man with a full beard passed by it. His appearance was stocky and rugged, but he didn't appear hostile toward her. The light eventually went off and shortly after, another turned on upstairs. Moments later her blonde hair appeared in the upstairs window. She sat in front of a mirror, tilting her head as the man followed her, kissed her on the cheek, and proceeded to pace towards the window Henry was spying through to close its blinds.

"You know," Henry said, his voice tinged with regret as he confided in Thomas. "Part of me wanted to cut ties with her, given how she deceived me. But I didn't. I let the affair go on because I was in love with her."

The Story of Cindy: Part 3

After the discovery, Henry stopped asking about Cindy's private life. His intuition led him to believe that she was fully aware that he knew of the affair. So, as he viewed it, they were both guilty of the arrangement, although neither of them admitted to it. This was fine for Henry—until it wasn't.

A disturbing knock on the door woke him from an afternoon slumber. The rap was frantic and loud.

"Hold on," he said as he tucked in his shirt.

"Oh. It's you," he said as he examined Cindy's worried face.

"What's wrong?" He mumbled groggily, rubbing the sleep away from his eyes.

"What's wrong? What do you think is wrong? Are you daft? Hurry up and get dressed. I have a cab waiting."

He didn't question her at first. He grabbed his wallet and keys and dashed down the stairs, following his lover into the back of the cab.

"What the hell's going on?" He turned to his distraught lover.

"He knows." She made no attempt to face him, her eyes were glued to the windshield.

He knew he was going to get blasted for playing dumb, but continued with his inquiry anyway. "*Who* knows?"

"Don't be an ass. You know as well as I do. My husband." She turned to face him finally. "Don't play that 'I didn't know' bullshit with me. You knew all along."

Henry looked away but didn't respond. He knew he had no one to blame but himself. Shortly thereafter, another feeling took over.

"What is he going to do? Come after me?"

"Yes!" Cindy affirmed, her tone sharp and urgent.

"What?"

"He'll never touch me, but he won't stand another . . ." Cindy stopped mid-sentence and leaned forward to gain the cabbie's attention. "Turn back please."

The driver nodded and clicked his turn signal.

"Henry." She pleaded to him. "It was wonderful and all. But we're done. I need to make it work with him. I'll try and persuade him to just leave it, but I don't think he'll listen. He's going to come for you. He's an undercover cop," Cindy explained urgently, her words laden with concern.

Henry's hand shot to his forehead in frustration. "For fuck's sake," he muttered under his breath.

"He had me followed," Cindy continued, her voice trembling slightly. "Do yourself a favor and get the hell out of town for a while."

He nodded, "OK." He remained stunned, not taking his eyes off the stained floor of the cab until it stopped. The only thing that came to him as parting words was, "I love you."

"Goodbye Henry."

He leaned toward her, but she recoiled, her eyes pleading with him to let her go. "Don't. Just go, please."

Henry left the cab, closing the door behind him as it sped off up the street.

From that very moment, the feeling of being watched began.

Once he got home he raced up the stairs to his apartment and immediately locked the door behind him. "Holy shit. I'm screwed," he muttered, the weight of the situation sinking in.

He slid gingerly toward the window, pulling the blinds shut before peeking out between the slats, searching for a black Crown Victoria - nothing in sight.

He rushed to his bedroom closet where he pulled out his suitcase and filled it with random clothes. Lastly, he rummaged through his dresser for his mother's new address printed on an envelope. The last items added were a notepad and pen. He latched it shut and called a cab.

"You're probably wondering why I grabbed the pad and pen." Henry began, his voice shaky with emotion.

Thomas nodded.

“I figured I was a dead man. Although I still felt the sting of what just happened, it finally occurred to me how awful it must have been for Angie when I left her. At least Cindy said goodbye. I didn’t even . . .”

Thomas didn’t answer. He waited for the man to manage his emotions.

“So, I wrote a letter to Angie while at the train station. I hid in a corner, away from everyone, hunched over like a terrified animal, wondering if that bald-headed-bearded husband of hers was going to shoot me down at Union Station.” Henry exhaled deeply before turning to Thomas. “Yeah, I had the shit scared out of me. Man-oh-man, I was terrified.”

“You didn’t see him?” Thomas inquired.

“I *did* see someone that looked just like the man I saw through the bedroom window. I saw him just before I boarded the train.”

“And the letter? What are you going to do with that?”

“Mail it, of course! My mom’s got her address at home. I’ll send it when I get to Victoria.”

Chapter 9 (Thomas)

4:30 pm CST - Saskatoon

I sat there, utterly speechless. I felt so naïve listening to this man talking about his love affair with the married woman. I realized for the first time how inexperienced I was. I hadn't even experienced love, let alone lust. I had no idea what he was feeling. I couldn't even empathize with him.

As the time passed on, so did the scenery outside my window. I relished in watching the western landscape pass by me. I became increasingly acquainted with my friend, the glowing sun. I was so thankful I chose a seat facing west.

I continued to scan the outdoor scenery, and I watched the landscape transition from vast expanses of golden wheat fields to quaint towns and eventually, a city. The train began to decelerate until it came to a halt at Saskatoon station.

10:30 pm CST

(Somewhere between Saskatoon and Edmonton)

I continued to immerse myself in the pages of Hemingway for hours until my exhaustion weighed heavy on me and I could no longer keep my eyes open. Reluctantly, feeling the strain of the day caught up to me, so I set the book aside, carefully arranging myself across the seats as I usually did and closed my eyes.

As I rested on those train seats, I opened my eyes every few minutes to check if Henry was asleep. Bit by bit, I noticed his chest move in and out as his breathing changed. He had a sort of happy expression about him while he slept. It was as if he was having a sweet dream. Maybe he was feeling comforted by Angie. Yes, Angie. I could imagine him lying there with his head on her lap as she stroked his forehead, pushing his hair away from his face, caressing it with her gentle touch.

Monday, August 17th -- 4:30 am MST (Edmonton)

I stirred from a deep slumber as the train came to a stop. The lights from the train station lit up the windows, causing me to open my eyes briefly to see Henry across from me still asleep. His mouth was open slightly and a little bit of drool was running from it. A few passengers boarded our train car, but I lay still. My eyes remained closed so that they wouldn't disturb me or have me sit up. As a few people boarded, I heard the soft shuffle of footsteps and I cracked my eyes just enough to glimpse a woman slipping past our section, balancing a baby in one arm and gripping the hand of a tired toddler with the other.

"I'm tired, Mommy," the child murmured.

"Shhhhhh. I know, honey," came the hushed reply from the weary mother.

At first, I was worried that they would keep us up all night, but they didn't—I was so tired that I slept through any noise they might have made.

As my eyelids became heavier and heavier, I noticed a bright red toy ball roll underneath where Henry was sleeping. The ball rolled a little more and then got stuck by the post that supported the row of seats underneath my friend. I tiredly watched as a tiny hand stretched out from under the seats trying to make contact with it.

7:30 am

(Somewhere between Edmonton and Jasper)

I woke up with the early morning sun poking through the south windows of the train. I glanced over at Henry, who to my surprise was still asleep. It was odd considering he usually awoke before I usually did. Perhaps it was earlier than I had realized, so I closed my eyes once more and drifted back into a state of unconsciousness.

As some time passed, I eventually sat up as I didn't need the rest, but the man across from me was still lying on his side. *He must have been really tired.*

I was momentarily distracted by a serviceman from the rail company traveling from the adjoining car into ours.

After he passed me, I rose from my seat and my eyes were fixed on Henry, who lay still and unmoving. A sense of unease crept over me as I crouched down and edged closer to him.

"Henry?" I called out lightly. The sound of my own voice echoed in my head. But as the words left my lips, a sudden chill shot through me. A shroud of fear enveloped me as I recoiled, stumbling backward in shock. "Oh, my God!" I gasped, the words escaping me in a panicked whisper.

The mother from the end of the train stood with her baby in her arms.

"Is anything the matter, sir?" Asked the serviceman.

I stood frozen, my hand trembling as I pointed towards Henry. "Something's wrong with him," I managed to utter.

The serviceman swiftly knelt beside Henry, his face grave as he attempted to rouse him. "Sir!" He called out urgently, his tone growing more insistent. "Sir!"

The serviceman touched his hand with his fingers, then turned.

"He's ice cold."

Without hesitation, the serviceman sprang into action, darting to the other side of the train to reach for his radio, "Stephen?" He spoke into the device.

A brief moment passed before a response crackled through the radio. "Stephen here."

"We need to stop the train," the serviceman relayed, his tone urgent and commanding.

I stood in the aisle in shock; completely numb as I examined Henry's lifeless body, his hand still clenching his jacket.

I could feel the train slow as I heard conversations over the radio.

"Do you know this man?" the serviceman asked.

I shook my head, my throat tight with emotion. "Yes, I mean... No, I don't know him. But I had been talking to him."

"He's not a relative or a friend?" he pressed.

"No, sir," I replied, my voice barely a whisper amidst the unfolding chaos.

"What's going on?" the mother asked, her gaze shifting between the serviceman and me.

"I believe this man passed away in his sleep."

"Oh, my God. I'm so sorry," the mother offered, her expression filled with compassion as she turned to face me.

The train finally came to a stop in the middle of a field with no buildings or roads in sight. The train car doors opened. The serviceman walked out of the car, waved towards the engine and stepped back on. After a few minutes, a man and a woman came into the car and surrounded Henry.

"Let's clear the car, please," The man announced, his tone authoritative as he examined the body and his hands clad in protective gloves.

I felt a shiver run down my spine as I watched his movements, the gravity of the situation sinking in.

"Ma'am, I'm sorry," the serviceman addressed the woman, his voice gentle yet firm. "I have to ask you to change cars. We can go through here for now."

The woman nodded silently, her expression filled with sadness as she gathered her things, her movements slow and deliberate.

Turning to me, the man's gaze met mine. "Sir, can you grab your belongings, please?" He requested.

I reached for my bag and turned to take one last look at Henry before I followed the mother and her two children through to the next car.

The serviceman directed us to where there were free seats. The woman sat with her baby and young boy in the middle of the car. I was taken farther down the car where I was placed across from a white-haired man. I was now facing the east.

"What's going on?" The old man piped up, his voice carrying a slight accent that I couldn't quite place.

I turned to him, noticing the concern etched on his weathered face. "A man died in his sleep," I replied somberly.

"Oh!" His eyebrows shot up in surprise, and he shook his head slowly. "What a shame," he murmured, his tone heavy with sympathy. "Was he an elderly man?"

"No. He was forty-five."

"That's young! The white-haired man had thick black eyebrows which poked out from above his gold-rimmed bifocals. When he spoke, a gold tooth situated on the bottom row of his teeth flashed—I found it distracting.

"I met him on the train in Toronto." I paused in thought. "I . . ." I started but couldn't continue.

Without warning, I began to experience incredible sorrow. The doors closed and the train eventually pulled us along the track, its speed about half of what it normally was.

As the train gently rocked back and forth, I looked out at the flat landscape without really taking it in.

After thirty minutes, the train slowed again. Some small buildings and houses began to dot the landscape more and more until it stopped at a station called Edson. Beside the building were an ambulance and a police vehicle, both with their lights flashing. Alongside the track were an officer and two men standing beside a stretcher waiting for the train to come to a halt. Once it did, I witnessed them enter the train car. This continued as the other members of the staff entered and exited the car. After twenty minutes or so, I followed the movement of the men carrying a large black bag and placing it on the stretcher, which was when passengers gasped, followed by a low rumble of chatter throughout the train car. The man across from me stood and turned to have a look.

"Oh, my goodness. What a shame," he uttered, sinking back into his seat with a solemn shake of his head.

Shortly after, the man with the radio entered the car and made his way toward our section.

"Excuse me, sir," he addressed me, "The officer would like to ask you a few questions before the train departs."

I nodded, rising from my seat, but hesitated. "The train won't leave without me, will it?" I asked, a hint of concern in my voice.

"No, sir."

"Don't worry, I'll save your seat," chimed in my newfound train companion.

I followed the rail employee until he introduced me to the officer.

"This is the young man who was seated across from the deceased," he explained.

"Right!" said the officer as he took out his notebook. "This will only take a few minutes. My name is Officer Murphy." He paused and jotted some notes. "Can you tell me what you know about this man and what happened the night before his death?"

I stood stunned for a moment as I could see the ambulance attendant loading Henry's body into the back of the ambulance and closing its doors.

"Sir?" asked the officer.

"Uhm . . . well . . . I met him at Union Station in Toronto when the train departed. I believe he lived in the east end of the city, I thought he said the beaches, but I'm not sure . . ."

"Where was he traveling to? Did he care to mention?"

"Victoria. He said something about his mother being ill and was going to rent a car from Vancouver to Victoria."

"Was there anything he would have said or shared with you that gave you the impression he was ill himself?"

"No. He seemed fine."

I answered a few more questions, then gave the officer my full name, address, and telephone numbers of my mother's home and my friend's home in Vancouver, in case they had any further questions. He gave me a card that listed the local police department's phone number. The officer thanked me for my time and then I returned to the train car.

When I re-entered, I passed along a section where there sat a bald man who sported a beard, but he didn't glance up at me when I passed. I didn't notice him earlier while I was being escorted to the car. I guess I was still in shock at that time. *Strange. I can't imagine that was the man following Henry. I must be carrying his paranoia now too.*

The train eventually left Edson station. I sat quietly looking east, which I didn't particularly like as I was essentially riding backward. The man across from me remained silent for hours, lost in his thoughts. Occasionally, he would doze off, his head nodding forward before he caught himself. It wasn't until we reached Jasper that he stirred from his sleep.

11:30 am MST – Jasper

As the train pulled away from the station, I made a conscious effort to distract myself from the recent tragedy by immersing myself in my book. However, I was interrupted by the man across from me, who rose from his seat with a slight grunt, "Excuse me."

I watched as he walked into the adjoining train car. He moved with a slight limp. I returned to the book and continued for twenty minutes until I lost focus of the story as my mind wandered off. As I sat, I began to think of death and what it meant. *Who called Henry's number? Why did he have to go now? Was he in poor health? Was there something else he wasn't telling me? Of course. He barely knew me, but then again, he did spill his guts. He told me some very personal stories. How does one qualify one's life after something like this? Did he live a good life? Was it bad? Oh yeah. He made his mistakes, though, didn't he?* I thought of everything he did on the train car and the things he claimed he hadn't done. *He never did venture to Europe to experience new cultures like he said I should. What if I only live to be forty-five?*

As the memory of Henry ran through my mind, I began to feel genuine pain and loss. My silly experiment to find temporary stimulation ended in me finding a friend, or more like an older brother. And then suddenly, he was taken away for no apparent reason. I was having difficulty pushing down my sorrow but was thankfully interrupted once again.

"I brought you some soup," the man said, his arm extended towards me, holding a container.

I accepted the container along with a plastic spoon.

"Thank you," I replied, my voice shaky with emotion.

"I thought you could use something to eat. It's been a tough day," he added sympathetically, removing the lid from his own container.

I held the warm container in my hand for a moment, not knowing what to do as I wasn't all that hungry. The man across from me took his first spoonful. "Go on. Get something into you," the man insisted.

I opened it, took a spoonful, and cooled it with my breath. The soup hit the spot. I needed something filling as I was feeling exhausted and weak, but it also temporarily took my mind off this morning's events. The old man across from me took sips, slurping every once in a while.

“You know,” the man said as he finished a spoonful. “We all have to deal with loss,” he murmured, carefully placing the lid back on his empty container, holding it in his hand. I’ve dealt with it recently. My wife passed away three months ago. We had been together for forty-one years. She was sixty-one when she passed. Not very old at all. This trip was planned for the two of us.” The man sighed with a pause, peered out at the scenery, then stood, motioning for me to pass my empty container.

“I’ll throw that out for you.”

He limped his way to the back of the car to dispose of the trash, and returned to his seat. He looked past me out of the window. A slow curve formed at the end of his lips, his gold tooth poking through. "Yes. This is what I came for, the Rocky Mountains. It’s so beautiful," he said, sporting a radiant smile.

I turned around, then back to the man with the gold-rimmed glasses. "May I ask your name, sir?"

"It’s George."

"Nice to meet you, George. I’m Thomas," I said, extending my hand, which he took, giving it a firm shake.

"Likewise."

"If you don’t mind me asking," I continued, "are you retired?"

"Oh, no . . ." George shifted in his seat. "I don't ever plan on retiring. I'm a barber. I've been cutting hair since I was twelve."

"Wow... So you started young then?"

"I did, indeed," George chuckled. "My father had me standing on crates in his barbershop, cutting customers' hair."

He had me thinking... "Where's that?"

"Qormi, a small town in Malta. That's where I'm from."

"I've heard of Malta. Where is it?"

"A small island, just south of Sicily."

"Do you speak Italian?"

"No. Maltese." The man grinned.

"Oh." I'm sure I blushed with embarrassment, so I changed the subject quickly to avoid becoming completely red in the face.

"My mother goes to a hairdresser."

The man smiled as if a thought had just occurred. "Do you know what the difference is between a barber and a hairdresser?" George asked.

I knew a joke of some sort was in the works. "No."

“About fifty bucks.” He chuckled, causing wrinkles around his eyes to form. The gold tooth made another appearance.

"That’s a good one," I chuckled, appreciating the humor in George's remark. "That would explain why my mom makes such a big deal about it." I leaned back against the train seat.

“You could use a haircut, yourself.”

"I know," I admitted with a sheepish grin, running my hand through my unruly hair.

As we bantered back and forth, a rail employee hurried past us through the center aisle of the train car.

"Excuse me," George called out, raising his voice slightly to catch the employee's attention.

The rail employee paused and turned towards us, giving George a questioning look. "Sir?"

George straightened up, "When’s the next stop?"

The employee turned and pulled his wristwatch from under his sleeve. “It’ll be in Kamloops. Another seven . . . seven and a half hours.”

George continued, still twisted in his seat as he spoke to the man. “How long will the train be stopped for?”

"’Bout an hour," he replied, his tone matter-of-fact. "The dining car needs to reload."

“Thank you,” George, the barber, said with a thoughtful nod. He reached into his jacket pocket to pull out an unfiltered cigarette. He proceeded to bang it on the case he retrieved, to knock the tobacco tighter. He then squinted as he lit it. When he inhaled, it appeared to give him some sort of comfort. I could never fully understand the nicotine fix.

He exhaled and offered: “I’ll give you a haircut when we stop.”

"Really?"

"Of course! Unless... you don’t want one." George shrugged.

I considered his proposition for a moment, realizing that a haircut would be a welcome change. "Yeah. I need one," I admitted.

George chuckled at my response, a slight cough escaping him as he struggled to contain his amusement. "I thought so too."

Suddenly, I felt a wash of anxiety over me, “I don’t have a lot of cash on me.”

"Oh, don’t worry about that," the man reassured me, waving away my concern with a casual flick of his hand.

The conversation seemed to stop and George took little puffs of his cigarette. He performed the task casually, enjoying the few minutes of pleasure it gave him. He was thinking to himself much like Henry would, which made me think of Henry's full moon story.

"Silly question for you," I asked, feeling a twinge of curiosity bubbling up inside me.

It appeared that I had interrupted the barber's concentration. He looked at me, raising a brow in inquisition. "What's that?" he asked, squishing his cigarette into the ashtray attached to the armrest, the faint scent of smoke lingering in the air.

"I found it interesting that the man I met had several stories about a full moon," I explained, "Do you have one, by chance?"

Nostalgia flickered in the Barbers' eyes. George leaned forward to straighten his shirt that was stuck to his seat. He grinned for a moment before answering.

"I do, as a matter of fact. But..." A contemplative look crossed his face.

"Yes?" I eagerly prompted.

"You might not believe it when I tell you."

"I gotta hear this," I insisted, sitting up straighter in the chair, leaning slightly.

Chapter 10

Jim Ferguson's last Haircut

(As recollected by George the Barber)

"I'll be back in an hour, Shirl," George called out as he let the screen door close behind him.

George thought to himself, *Shirley never complained when I went out in the evening to cut one of my customer's hair; especially while in the hospital. She never asked, but she knew I didn't accept any money.*

Many times, George would grab his weathered brown leather pouch of tools which contained the perfect set-up. He kept two pairs of scissors, an electric trimmer, a straight razor, a hairbrush, and a barber's cape. He drove across town in his 1975 Green Ford LTD, peering up at the night sky, lit by the full moon. Once he reached Toronto General Hospital, he strode toward the main entrance with his pouch neatly tucked under his arm. It was customary for him to wear a suit jacket to and from work. When he reached his barbershop, he quickly shed the jacket he wore and slipped into his stark white barber jacket, ready to greet his customers. However, he kept his regular jacket on when he arrived at the hospital.

"Mr. Jim Ferguson," the barber said while leaning over the reception desk.

The woman pushed her chin into her chest and quickly checked her watch. "It's quarter to eight. You've got fifteen minutes, sir. Our visiting hours are almost over. Room 209 to your right."

"That's all right," he replied. "I'm just going to have him sign this form," he said, patting his pouch, darting towards the elevator.

The receptionist grumbled something under her breath as he whisked himself away.

"Hello, Jim. How are you feeling?" He murmured while passing through the door.

George did his best to conceal his surprise at how much Jim Ferguson deteriorated since he last cut his hair. He was much thinner and his complexion had changed to a death-like gray. The ill man was gaunt, barely a hundred pounds.

He huffed, "About as good as one can be when filled with cancer."

George didn't respond but proceeded to remove his suit jacket and spread out his tools onto the side table.

"Are you feeling up to it? I can come back another time," George offered.

Jim smacked his dry lips before speaking, his voice hoarse but determined. "You're a good man for coming, George. Nope. There won't be another time. So, get on with it. This is my casket haircut,"

"Now, don't say that, Jim. I'll be back in a month," George reassured him, trying to lighten the mood.

"And, you're gonna take my money this time," Jim added with a weak chuckle.

"OK," George grinned as he gently placed the cape around his customer's neck, knowing full well he wasn't going to be taking a dime.

"Who came by today?" George asked. "I don't like to come too early, as I don't want to disturb your family visits."

Jim Ferguson didn't respond.

A beep came through the hospital intercom: "Ladies and gentlemen. Visiting hours are now over."

George waited for a response before repeating his question, “I said . . .”

“I heard ya the first time, George.”

“Jeez. I’m just asking.” George maintained his composure, being patient with the man who was not himself.

“George?”

“Yes, Jim?” the barber replied, placing the comb and scissors to the man’s head, maneuvering it through his hair.

"Have you ever seen my family any time you’ve come?"

The barber paused briefly, “I can’t say that I have," he admitted. "That’s why I come later on."

The room became silent with the exception of the scissors snipping away.

Jim cleared his throat before continuing. “Family don’t come to see me.”

“Oh, come on now, Jim. I’m sure they do.” George carried on, lifting the thin and ailing man’s hair with his comb as he snipped.

“They’ve disowned me years ago. Don’t talk to me no more,”

George pulled his arms away from his client before replying, "Is there something you want to tell me?"

"As a matter of fact, I do." He murmured heavily.

George returned to where he left off, tilting his head slightly as he peered through the bottom of his bifocals.

Jim started, "You know me as just ol' Jim the customer, don't ya George?"

"I wouldn't say that. You've been a good friend *and* customer."

Jim let out a rueful chuckle, though it was strained and weak. "Huh! You don't know the half of it! I am not a good man. To anyone that really knows me. I'm not a good man."

George circled the hospital bed and started with the other side of the man's head, saying nothing but, "Tilt your head a little for me, please. There."

"Julie, my wife, she…," Jim confessed, his voice tinged with remorse. "She put up with my bullshit for nearly forty years – my drinkn', my running around with other women. I was a terrible husband I tell ya. Why I once took a trip with the boys and spent twenty grand in one week. Twenty grand,

George!" His words were laced with self-condemnation. "That was my first introduction to coke. Ever did coke before?" He asked, his eyes searching the barber's face for a reaction.

The barber shook his head, maintaining an expressionless face.

"Had to remortgage the house. Nathan had to quit university. And you know what?"

"What's that?"

"I never once apologized to any of 'em. Not once! Too proud. Yes, sir. Too fuckin' proud."

Jim smacked his cracking lips and continued with a huff, "I had me many women while I was married. Yes, sir. I figured Julie knew all along. She never said nothin'"

The room remained silent except for George's feet shuffling around the bed and the snipping of his instrument.

"Nathan got a girlfriend and moved out. Got a job making good money. Then went back to university to continue what he started. Graduated from law school. Did pretty well too, so I hear. I never went to his graduation. Was fishin' in Cuba with the boys."

Jim continued while George worked and snipped, "One day, I'd say, a year or so ago, Julie and I were sittin' on the back deck, sipping our wine and I says, 'Honey. Why doesn't our boy come and see us anymore? He too good for us now or somethin'?'"

"The wife says to me, 'He does, Jim. Just not when you're around.' I says 'What the hell's that supposed to mean? Are you tellin' me Nathan's comin' to see you . . . only when I'm not around?' Julie said yes, then . . . you know what she said then, George?" His voice got louder and more upset.

"What's that, Jim?"

"She said . . . she said she stopped lovin' me' years ago. She had been faking her love the last… twenty freakin' years. All of it, fake."

"Can you move your head, just a little . . ." George touched the back of Jim's head gently. "That's it." The barber twisted himself to cut at an awkward angle.

"I didn't believe her. No, I sure didn't. "I figured she was just pissed off at me for the fishin' trip and missin' the boy's grad. Well . . . I was sure wrong about that. Not long after,

I was diagnosed with cancer. Julie seemed upset at first, but something changed. Something wasn't right. I guess. . . I guess that's when it kicked in." Jim paused, his voice cracking as he struggled to continue.

"Well . . . just to tell you how much she meant it when she said she didn't love me, she came with me the first day I was admitted. Before she left, she sat down nice and close to me and said: '*Jim. I don't know what to tell ya. You've been a selfish man all your life. I wish you no sufferin'. I'll manage just fine without ya when you're gone. I wish you peace in your next life, Jimmy.*' Then, she was gone." Jim's voice crackled, which was followed by a wet cough.

"And Nathan?" George asked. "I'm sure he will visit."

"He hates my guts." Jim almost went to shake his head. "Julie made a point of tellin' me. She didn't keep it no secret."

George let out a sigh, "I'm sorry to hear this." He turned to cut the top of his client's head, taking a moment to brush the excess hair from Jim's forehead before finishing the top.

"Don't be," Jim Ferguson disagreed. "I made my own bed. Now here I am. Dying with no one around; no one to even take pity on me."

The hallway lights turned off, causing the barber to look out the door before continuing.

"Jeez! I'd better hurry before they kick me out," George replied.

Snip, snip, snip, was all that could be heard for the next few minutes until Jim interrupted the rhythm.

"George, there's twenty bucks in the top drawer. Be a pal and take it, please." Jim uttered, his voice growing weaker. The barber grinned to himself, touched by Jim's gesture.

"You're not gonna take it, are ya?" Jim asked.

George shook his head, still sporting his grin. "No, Jim. I won't take it,"

After a few moments of silence, the ailing man asked with his voice barely above a whisper, "George?"

"Yes, my friend," George looked at him while he replied.

"Do you believe in the afterlife?"

The barber hesitated before responding, his hands motionless before he said, "I never used to. But, now that I'm older, I believe there's something out there. So, yes," George replied thoughtfully, his gaze drifting to the window as if searching for answers in the darkness of night. "I can't say what that is, though."

Jim nodded slowly. He coughed harshly and mucus dribbled down his quivering chin.

"Pass me a tissue, would you?" He pointed weakly to his bedside.

George reached for the tissue box and handed one to Jim.

The sick man dabbed the soiled area before George brushed the remaining pieces of hair off of Jim's ears and delicately reached around the client's neck to unclasp the cape, being careful not to spill the collection of hair.

The barber shook the cape into the garbage can and meticulously placed all his tools back in his leather pouch. He checked his watch but didn't leave. Instead, he slid his suit jacket over his shoulders and brought a chair up to his sickly client.

"Jim, can I ask ya something?" He looked over to his client.

He lightly shrugged his shoulders.

"Do you… Do you regret the things you've done?"

Jim tried to speak but his words were too gargled and labored to understand. George raised his hand to stop him from straining as his client was obviously exhausted from the conversation.

"Just nod, OK, Jim?." He took a slow breath. "Do you regret the things that you've done to your wife and son?"

He nodded, his eyes watered.

"When I leave this room, confess your sins. Confess your sins and God will forgive you. We've all made mistakes. I've certainly made my own," George urged with quiet intensity.

Jim nodded solemnly with shame, his head downcast.

George slid the leather pouch from off of the side table and tucked it under his arm.

"You're a good man, Jim. *I* think so," he placed his hand on his client's frail arm. "Remember what I said."

Jim Ferguson didn't say anything, and out of room 209 George the barber went.

The aging barber took a few steps into the hallway and stopped. He scanned the dark passage from left to right before cautiously taking his next steps. The hallway wasn't only dark but was incredibly quiet. The shuffling of his shoes echoed against the shiny floors and brick hallways until he stopped in front of an open door.

The barber stood still, taking in the image of a boy of around seven years of age, kneeling, his eyes closed as he prayed. The boy wore a suit jacket, shorts, and white socks pulled to his knees. His dark hair was combed perfectly. While the boy prayed, a priest on the other side of the partition delivered a quote in Latin.

Although George recognized the boy, he didn't stop. He clutched his pouch and scurried out the doors as quietly as possible.

Chapter 11 (Thomas)

“There wasn’t a soul in sight—not a nurse, a doctor, a utility man. There was no one.” George said.

“Was that . . . was that a chapel in the hospital that you passed?” I asked, quietly.

“No. That was me, as a boy. And that was no hospital. Something happened that night, something unexplainable. When I left Jim Ferguson’s room, something happened to me. I stumbled into my own journey through some sort of purgatory. Except, I hadn’t died. It was very strange. That was no hospital. No, sir. I was somewhere else.”

I sat there, stunned at the strangeness of the barber’s story as we sat there in eerie tension.

"I told you. You wouldn't believe me. Not even if ya tried." The barber confidently remarked.

"I didn't say that," I responded, feeling a need to reassure him, though uncertainty gnawed at the edges of my mind.

“I will tell you though...” The barber adjusted himself in his seat, “I’ve been to Toronto General before and since that visit, and nothing like that ever happened. Never before and never again."

"That's a pretty creepy story." I felt myself unable to shake off the unsettling feeling that lingered afterward. He made me feel like Henry did.

"But I learned from it," the barber continued.

"How so?"

"Jim Ferguson paid for his sins. Not in the afterlife, but while living. I believe he did ask for forgiveness before he passed. As for me. I knew that was me as a little boy in Malta, taking my first communion. I witnessed myself as an innocent child, which made me reflect on all of *my...* sins. And . . ." George removed another cigarette from his side pocket, banged it on the case before stealthily lighting it. "Shortly after, I made a point of making a better effort to always be respectful of my family. I practiced patience and understanding. When my wife was ill and eventually passed, there was no remorse, no regrets." George's eyes locked with mine, causing me to look away awkwardly. "When my time comes, I hope to feel the heavens and not the heaviness of what hell can bring to a man before and in the afterlife."

I nodded.

The rest of the afternoon I thought about what the barber had told me. Although I wasn't sure if I understood what happens in the afterlife or even in his "real-life-purgatory," I do believe things happen for a reason. I *do* believe in fate.

I studied the scenery for hours contemplating it all. Then something happened to me. I began to focus on myself and what kind of life I was going to live. My thoughts about the future changed. They changed from hoping for something to happen, to taking steps to do it.

I am going to go to Europe; I am going to go to Gorizia, Milan, and Stresa, and I will ask a young lady out on a date instead of waiting for her to knock on my door. I've been too passive. I can't keep going year after year as a bystander to my own life.

I opened my book to where I had left off, removed the bookmark, and returned to page one. *I'm going to read this novel with a different frame of mind.*

7:30pm PST - Kamloops

After dinner, the train arrived in Kamloops just as the sun was about to go down, casting a warm glow over the landscape outside.

"See that chair there on the platform?" George asked as he peered out the window.

"Yes?

"Go and sit on it before somebody takes it. I'll be out in a moment," George instructed while gesturing for me to make my way to the coveted seat.

As I was getting up, George turned to the passengers on the other side of the aisle and politely asked them to watch our things.

I stepped off the train and made my way to the chair, settling into its worn wooden frame as I waited for George to join me on the platform. "Could ya pull it away from the fence?" George called out to me.

I nodded, grasping the chair and dragging it a few feet away from the iron fence that lined the platform, ensuring a clear view of the passing trains and the vibrant sunset.

He peered up at the beautiful orange sky, where the silhouette of the mountains perfectly situated. “We’re lucky. Sun’s just about to go down, but we still have enough light.” He wrapped the cape around me.

Part of me felt silly getting a haircut on the platform in front of all the on-lookers from the train, but that didn’t matter. I mean, how often do you get to meet a nice old man willing to give you a free haircut?

No, I didn’t feel silly. I was *honored*.

“So, Thomas, you got a girlfriend back home?”

"No, sir. No girlfriend.” I heard the zipper run and there I saw a handy, carry-on kit. There lay three different kinds of scissors, a black tail comb, a fluffy brush and a plastic cape.

“What’s taking you to Vancouver then?” He questioned, preparing his scissors above my hair, “Sightseeing? A friend?”

"An old friend. He moved out there years ago. I haven't seen him in ten years. It's going to be..." I paused in thought, "something for sure."

The barber slid the soles of his shoes along the platform pavement as he continued to snip his scissors above my head. I found it humorous that he treated me like a customer as soon as that barber cape went on, he had so many questions that kept the conversation going.

"Do you play sports? Have any hobbies?"

"I play badminton at a local club. My uncle David introduced me to it," I replied casually.

"Ah," George responded mechanically, though his attention seemed elsewhere for a moment. "And your parents? What do they do?"

"Just my mom. I never knew my dad," I cleared my throat awkwardly; George didn't seem to notice.

"I see."

"Mom works at the Chrysler trim plant in Ajax," I added to stray from the subject of my father.

"She works for the Big Three. That's a good job. And you? What will your career be?"

"I don't know yet. Part of the reason I took this trip was to sort of . . . clear my head of things at home. Not that there is anything wrong there. I just needed to get away."

"I was eighteen when I left Malta," George interjected, "I also know what it's like to be so far away from home and family. I had many lonely nights, but you survive like I did. I had to learn your language, mind you," he added with a wistful smile.

"You speak perfect English," I added. "You barely have an accent."

"Straighten your head just a little . . ." the barber said. "There!"

George bent his knees, finding the perfect angle, as I'm sure the height of the chair wasn't ideal.

"Whatever you do. I mean . . ." George continued while he worked. "Whatever occupation you take up, make sure you enjoy it. As you've witnessed yourself, life can be short. Enjoy every day as if it's your last. That's been my outlook since that night at the hospital with Jim."

I didn't comment. The barber was now working the back of my head. I could feel the gentle lift of the comb followed by the snips. Once he finished the back, he shuffled around to my front and worked on top.

"Good for you for taking a big trip across the country like this, all on your own." He looked me in the eyes before going back to my hair. "Most kids your age wouldn't leave the comforts of their home."

"Thank you." I felt the need to say so.

Most of the passengers still on the train passively watched as the barber did his work. I could tell he took pride in it. His words of wisdom meant so much to me too. The feeling of knowing I wouldn't see him again once my trip was over upset me, but I hurriedly pushed that out of my mind. I didn't want to think about it.

"All done, my friend." I pressed my eyes shut as he brushed the hair off my forehead.

He removed the cape and finished by flapping it in the wind over the fence.

I stood while he crouched over his pouch that neatly displayed the tools he didn't use. He folded the cape into an eight-by-eight-inch square and placed it inside, pulling the zipper all the way 'round to shut it.

"Thank you," I said and followed the man back into the train car.

11:00 pm

With his glasses tucked in his jacket, George was fast asleep with his mouth open, the faint growl of a snore could be heard as he breathed.

It never occurred to me until that night how life can offer so many challenges to people, and still, they make the decisions that they do.

Was I so naïve that I never considered that individuals like Henry or even George's client, Jim Ferguson, would make decisions that could significantly change the outcome of their lives? How does that happen? I mean, I've been faced with decisions before, but I hadn't had to make one with any bearing on my life or others. Or have I? No. I don't think so.

The self-contemplation was hurting my brain, so I decided to open Hemmingway's novel and read about Lt. Fredrick Henry and his friend Rinaldi again. I read for some time until the end of Book 1 when I discovered how unusually dark the train was. The blackness made me feel lonely and insecure; the confidence and determination I had earlier had subsided. I felt like a young boy again, waiting for daylight to break onto the horizon.

I placed my book in my bag and reclined my seat all the way back, pulling my jacket to my chin. I tried to close my eyes but I couldn't help but notice the moon shining down on me from the eastern sky.

It wasn't a full moon anymore, but it was bright enough to poke through my eyelids. I was tired so I covered my head with my jacket. As I lay curled up in my seat, I let my body shift back and forth with the movement of the train until the rocking motion made me dozy. My tense muscles relaxed on the cushioned train seats as if I had taken a mild sedative. *Ahhh, this is nice*. I felt that I was floating just above my seat, barely touching it, but I wanted to see the moon.

I didn't want to hide from it anymore, so I pulled my jacket from my face, but to my surprise, in front of me stood the bearded bald man I saw when I re-entered the train that morning. He stood over me just watching, until he took action. He covered my mouth with one hand and brought the forefinger of his other to his lips indicating for me not to make a sound.

"Follow me," he whispered firmly. "And don't say a damn word."

I nodded quickly and I got off my seat.

"Grab your things," he suggested, low but harshly. "Through there," he muttered, pushing me from behind between the aisle of sleeping passengers.

We continued on and through the doors between the train cars until we reached the empty one where I first met Henry.

"All the way to the end," he spoke behind me a little louder now that we were alone. "That's it. Keep going. Right where you were the other day."

I took the seat where I had lived for the first three days of my journey. The stocky man with the beard took Henry's seat, plopping his imposing frame onto it.

"Now," he said, flipping his jacket to one side, exposing a handgun secured in its holster. "You're going to answer my questions with complete honesty. Got it?"

"Yes, sir." I nodded subordinately.

"Good," he replied with absolute authority. "Let's start with an easy one. You know who I am?"

"No," I answered.

The man lowered his head, seemingly annoyed. He let out a frustrated sigh. "Ok. Let's try this again. "Do you know who I am?"

"I—I think so."

"How about you take a really good guess." He lifted his chin and waited.

"You're . . . you're Cindy's . . . husband?" My brow rose as I asked insecurely.

The man produced a grin that was all but friendly.

"And how would you know a thing like that?"

I pointed to where he was sitting, "Henry told me." I replied evenly, trying to remain calm.

Just as I pointed, I noticed Henry's suitcase still underneath his seat, but I avoided drawing my eyes to it for fear the bearded man would notice.

"That's right. The Henry that couldn't keep his hands to himself. What else do you know about me?" His eyes narrowed as he scrutinized me.

"Um . . . I know that you're an undercover cop and that . . ." I hesitated, feeling the weight of his gaze bearing down on me.

"Go on," he urged, his tone insistent as he leaned in closer. Everything about him began to slowly intensify.

“And that you might be following him.”

“Now you’re talkin’. Don’t play games, OK? Just answer the questions,"

“O-OK."

“You were the last one to see him alive, weren’t you?”

“Yes, sir.”

“Yeah,” The man shifted in his seat, his eyes darting to the train car window before returning to me. “I saw you . . .” His voice trailing into a tense silence. “I saw you speaking with that local constable.”

I said nothing in response, my heart pounding in my chest as I waited for him to continue.

“And you got yourself a nice new haircut too, right in front of everyone to see, including me.”

I kept quiet.

“So? What did you tell the cop?”

“I said . . . I said that I knew him a little, that I had met him on the train, and . . . ah . . . that he must have died in his sleep.” My voice faltered slightly.

“And what else?” He prodded.

“I told him where I met him and where he was going,” I continued before I was interrupted.

"Where was he going by the way?" the burly man inquired.

"To Victoria. To see his mother."

"Awe, to go be with his mommy. Isn't that sweet?" The man scoffed sarcastically, cocking his head to one side.

I didn't reply.

"What else?"

His tone grew insistent, "You didn't mention anything about someone who may have been following him?"

"No."

"Are you sure?"

"No. I mean, yes. I'm sure."

"Did you mention you saw me?"

"No." I paused to think. "I didn't notice you until . . ."

It finally sunk in. The realization finally hit me. *He was in the next car all along. He must have had something to do with Henry's death. Henry didn't die from a heart attack. He was murdered!*

"That's right. You could still call the Edson police, once you arrive in Vancouver, couldn't you?"

The man flashed a nasty grin. *What does he want from me? Is he going to kill me now?*

No. I . . . I won't," I stammered and broke eye contact, unable to bear the intensity of his glare any longer.

"How do I know that?"

"I . . . I figured he died of a heart attack," I offered weakly, my gaze flickering back up to meet his own. "I'll just . . . stick with that story."

"I think you'd better. Does this address sound familiar?" The bearded man pulled a notepad from his jacket, "575 Admiral Road, Ajax."

My heart pounded in my chest as I recognized the address. "Yes," I admitted reluctantly.

"Yes, what?"

"That's... That's my address. My address back home." I cleared my throat in anxiety.

"Let me continue," His voice menacing and low, "And the woman who lives there . . . a Lesley Henry."

A sense of dread washed over me as I lowered my head. I was beyond worried now. This man knew where I lived and my mother's name.

"So, here's the deal, you don't change your story and I won't pay a visit to your mom. Sound fair?"

"Yes."

I sat silent again as the man continued. His eyes were still fixated on me. It was extremely uncomfortable and I wanted to run away like a small child.

"May I go now?"

"Nah." He shook his head. "I'm not done quite yet. I'm still on a mission."

I waited for him to continue.

"I love my wife, but I put her through the wringer pretty good too." He paused, still watching me. "She said that Henry fella had a woman friend, from a long time ago—another girl. I wonder what her name is." The man tilted his head, anticipating a response.

I shrugged my shoulders trying to lie the best I could. It was the only way I could try and honor Henry,

"Is your mother a good person, Thomas?"

"All right," I let up. "Her name is Angie Peterson."

"There. That wasn't so hard, was it? Angie Peterson," he repeated the name, jotting it down on his notepad.

"Where does she live?"

"Whitby," I hung my head.

"That's more like it."

Although I had difficulty making eye contact with the undercover cop, I couldn't look away as I was worried he would catch me eyeing the suitcase. That suitcase would probably have everything the bearded man needed: Angie's letter, his mother's address, Henry's address in Toronto, and maybe even Angie's address in Whitby. This jealous husband would wreak havoc on his family. *Don't look down.*

The empty train car jolted suddenly causing the bearded man to shift in his seat as he wrote.

He tucked the notepad and pen into his side pocket and maintained his expressionless face.

Don't look down, Thomas.

The man raised a brow in suspicion of my movements, "You're guilty." He concluded, "You're guilty of something."

"What? No. No, I'm not," I proclaimed my innocence vehemently. There was nothing that I was guilty of. "I've done nothing wrong."

"All I need is to find something on you and then . . . The handcuffs go on and you're all mine. Then . . . you'll have no chance of going to the cops about me," the bearded man threatened maliciously.

The man straightened himself in his seat, "Open your bag," he ordered, his voice cold and commanding as he pointed a finger in my direction.

"What?" I stammered.

“I said open your bag. I want to see what a young man has to travel with. I’ll find something. Every twenty-one-year-old has a joint or acid or something illegal,” he waited for my compliance.

I did as he asked, my hands shaking as I fumbled with the zipper of my bag. I dumped its contents onto the seat beside me, my heart racing with apprehension.

The man hovered over the pile, his hands sifting through it savagely. His eyes scanned for something incriminating.

"Well, what have we here?" He exclaimed holding up the copy of A Farewell to Arms. “Is this yours?”

I nodded, my throat tight with fear.

“Good book?” He asked while flipping through it.

I didn't answer him as I swallowed.

His eyes narrowed as he looked at the blue inscription on the inside cover. “It says here, Property of Ajax High School,”

“What? Oh, yeah. Ha,” I chuckled awkwardly as my cheeks burned.

“You’re twenty-one. You’re not in high school anymore. You should have returned this years ago! That’s theft,” The man accused.

“What? No! I just . . . forgot,” I protested at the argument.

"That's enough for me to arrest you." He glared at me with undisguised hostility.

"You can't arrest me for that!"

"You're under arrest for stolen property. Stand up! Stick your arms out." The man reached around his waist to grab his handcuffs. He stood, leaned over, and grabbed my arm firmly.

"No!" I yelled.

George released my arm, and I jumped in my seat, my heart racing with sudden fear as I blinked in the harsh light of day. The train had come to a stop, and the reality of our arrival jolted me out of my head.

"You were having a dream," George said gently, his voice pulling me back to the present as he stood over me, his expression kind yet concerned. "We're finally here."

I blinked again, trying to shake off the remnants of sleep still clinging to my senses. "Where are we?" I asked, my voice hoarse with disorientation.

Tuesday, August 18th -- Vancouver, 8:30 am PST

"Vancouver!" the barber said as he flashed his gold tooth. He leaned towards me, bowing slightly. "It was a pleasure meeting you, Thomas," he said, holding out his hand. "Enjoy your trip."

"Thank you for the haircut!"

I remained seated as passengers shuffled around the car, gathering their belongings. I leaned away from the seat, reaching around to feel my back drenched with sweat. *Holy! That was a crazy dream! It was incredibly surreal.*

I watched as George and all the other passengers filled the aisle and departed the train car, including the bald man. The bearded bald man didn't look back at me. He was less stocky and far less intimidating than in my dream. Once the aisle was almost empty, I put my jacket on, grabbed my bag, and stepped off the train onto the platform.

It felt a little bizarre to be on the ground again. My legs were wobbly and they nearly felt atrophied from the amount of time I had spent sitting on the train. I started to make my way towards the train station when I stopped and turned back to the infamous train car. *I wonder...*

I casually paced toward the car where there was no movement, which made sense as we'd evacuated it the day before. It was eerie when I entered, not only because of Henry's passing but also because of that awful dream I just had; however, to my astonishment, his suitcase was still tucked under the seat! *I can't believe it! The paramedics left his suitcase.* I snatched it and exited the train as casually as I could.

I made my way back onto the platform and down the stairs where I entered the station, which was peppered with small coffee shops, gift shops, and restaurants. As I scanned the interior, my eye caught a Budget Rental car counter which made me think of Henry. I decided to sit on a bench that was facing the street, contemplating if I should open Henry's suitcase. I knew it was wrong, and outlandishly personal to do, but the temptation of it poked at me as I could imagine the devil's bony finger would.

I slid the two buttons simultaneously inwards causing a *click* that was unusually loud. The contents were scrambled. Bit by bit I sifted through a pair of khakis, a white Arrow shirt, two Lacoste tennis shirts, boxers, socks, and a burgundy tie. In the lid of the suitcase were filled pockets, one of which contained several brown and white envelopes, one from a lawyer on Front Street and one written in perfect cursive from a Grace Thomas addressed to Henry Thomas. The return address was in Victoria and the envelope was torn open.

"Huh!" I exclaimed aloud. *His name is Henry Thomas. My name is Thomas Henry. Isn't that funny!*

I poked my fingers inside. It was a short letter addressed to him, dated September 1979.

Henry,

You know you are always welcome to stay with me. Take as long as you need to get back on your feet. I could always use the company, anyway. You don't need to fuss about money for anything. I will take care of that. Just be sure to wake up early and prepare that special breakfast you always make for me.

I will wire you the money for the train ticket on Wednesday. The bank says to give it a couple of days. I'm sure it will be in your account by the time you get my letter.

And for goodness sake, please stop stressing yourself! You sounded so uptight on the phone the last time we spoke. Once you settle your finances, you can find work here if you would like. It will all work out in the end, I am sure of it. All I ask is that you help me with the gardens in the fall and shovel the driveway for me in the winter. The boy across the road is sweet and all, but he's barely reliable.

Mrs. Geric's next door has a niece who is over from Hungary. She is single and Mrs. Geric's thinks you two may get along. I think she's a little younger, but I'm sure you could use the company of someone around your age.

I will see you on the 21st

Love,

Mom

I refolded the note and returned it to the torn open envelope.

There was another envelope that wasn't glued together or ripped open like the first. Inside was a perfectly folded hand-written letter. It read:

August 14, 1981

Dear Angie,

I can imagine you're shocked by the name on the return address. It took me far too many years to write this. I procrastinated, not only because I struggled with what to say, but the other half of me debated whether you'd already buried the thought of me years ago, and sending you this now would just cause you to hate me even more than you already do. I would understand if you did. But I made the decision, so here I am, sitting at Union Station, once again, writing a letter to the one woman I truly loved.

Yes, I admit that I was young and stupid, so painfully stupid. I was never raised to treat another human the way I did you. I am appalled and so ashamed of myself. If I had anything in life that was worth living for, I threw it all away that night that I left you. I walked away from my love and my child. You want to know when it hit me? It was when I sat down to dinner with my *mother and she asked me, 'Whatever happened to that Angie girl you were so fond of in your letter?' That's when it hit me the hardest. I was twenty-five hundred miles from you when the weight of it came crashing down. I deserve every bit of the guilt and shame.*

It wasn't just the realization of it, no... It's the memory of you that keeps popping up! I'm always reminded of you all the time, almost every day! Such as, whenever I hear the phrase 'hi, baby,' it reminds me of you, or when someone grabs two bottles of beer and they 'clink' together, it reminds me of our conversations at the kitchen table, or when I see a folded note left for a lover in a movie, it reminds me of you. That's right, you had that effect on me, more than any other woman had.

Still, though, I will be honest. I never told anyone about my leaving you, about leaving you with child. No, I was too worried about what people would think. I was too proud to tell anyone for fear they would think less of me. So, I lived with this, year after year.

I could go on and on about how reckless and thoughtless I was, but I will stop here as there is only one thing I want to say. I am truly sorry for what I did. I want you to know that you are the most wonderful woman

I have ever met and I wish you all the best this world has to offer.

With love,

Henry Thomas

While I sat, taking in his letter to Angie, I thought to myself: *This letter is never going to make it to her.* The realization of it saddened me.

I placed it back in the envelope and closed the suitcase. I temporarily forgot about my friend Cameron. He agreed to pick me up at the station, but he was nowhere in sight. I scanned the station but still, there was no twenty-one-year-old redhead to be seen. Across from me was a man, about my age standing inside a telephone booth, talking and laughing as he held the receiver between his neck and shoulder. I felt the need to call my mom and tell her everything that had happened in the last four days but what felt like a lifetime. O*nce that guy is finished, I'm going to call her.* That's when it hit me, how far away from home I was. Then came another knot in my stomach. *Maybe I will just stay a week instead of two. Yeah, that's what I'll do. I'll just tell Cameron something has come up and that I can only stay a week. I'm sure I can change the ticket easily.*

“Hey!” a young woman in front of me called out. “Weren’t you the guy getting a haircut on the platform in Kamloops?”

When I turned my head to see who was talking to me, I was caught off guard by her sudden appearance. “Yeah, that was me all right,” I grinned with pride. I drew a blank as to what to say next though.

“I was one of the people watching you from the train. Lucky guy you are!” She pointed to the bench beside me. “Is this seat taken?”

“No. “It’s all yours,” I said and shuffled myself over to the edge of it.

“Thanks.”

I continued waiting, straining my neck, looking out for Cameron.

“Wow, that was a long time on that train.”

“It sure was!”

“I mean, holy. I’ve taken the train before but this time, Jeez. My ass must have bruises on it from sitting for so long!” she continued with a soft chuckle. "Then... that poor guy, you know - the one that died in Alberta. Did you see that? I swear my train car was talking about it the rest of the trip." She sighed empathetically, pushing her hair from over her shoulder.

"Yeah... he was in my car. We spoke nearly the whole trip, till he-" I cut myself off. I didn't want to say it out loud.

Her eyes widened with shock and her shoulders shrunk into her small figure, "Really? That's horrible."

"Yeah. I had to meet with the police and everything." My eyes downcast, like they did in my dream, I was filled with the memories over the last several days. I felt like my life had changed. "That was a blur. I can hardly remember anything of what I said."

"Gosh, that's awful! Must've been terrible, I bet. Was he traveling with anyone else?"

"He was by himself. Just me and him when we left Union Station."

I studied the young woman's face while she peered down at her suitcase which was scraped and worn. She bore simple but pleasant features, such as her small but plump lips and a lightly freckled face. Her brown hair was silky smooth with a beautiful sheen. It was draped over her shoulders and onto the middle of her back. I would guess she was about my age.

"What brings you here?" she asked with sudden curiosity.

"A friend of mine. A longtime friend. He was supposed to be here by now, but . . .he's late." I studied the clock on a white pillar over by the inside of the station before peering back down at Henry's suitcase.

"Oh right, I better take this into the lost and found. Know where it is?" I looked at her, squinting my eyes from the bright sun.

"I sure do. Been here a million times. It's just over yonder," she pointed. "Is that . . . is that the man's suitcase?"

"Yeah. They left it on the train. Good thing I checked before I left."

"I'll say."

I stood up, but soon sat back down, feeling a sudden rush of nerves. After a moment of hesitation, I blurted out, "I'm Thomas by the way." I extended my hand to her.

"Lucy." She replied with a warm smile. "So, how does that happen?" She gestured towards my freshly cut hair and the suitcase in my hand.

"What do you mean?"

"You've had quite the experience. A man dies, then you have his suitcase, and then . . . like a celebrity, get a haircut on the platform of a train station!"

"Okay, well now I'm embarrassed," I replied sheepishly.

"Don't be. Everyone on the train was like, 'What a lucky fella. He must be a V.I.P. or something.'" She reassured me with another wave of her hand.

I slid my hand from my forehead down my face, shaking my head.

"His name was George... the barber, one of the nicest men I think I've ever met."

"Wow! You had quite the experience. Like . . . I didn't talk to anyone the whole time." She remarked.

"So back to you," I said, eager to shift the focus of our conversation. "What brings you all the way to Vancouver?"

"Actually. I'm waiting for a rental. They're still cleaning it. I rented a car to visit my aunt and uncle who live in Victoria. I've been here now . . . hmmmmmm . . . three times." She turned to me and her eyes sparkled from the sun. "You need a lift somewhere?"

"Oh, ah. Thanks, but Cameron is supposed to pick me up." I replied, my gaze scanning the bustling station in search of my red-headed friend. "I wonder where he is?"

It was silent for a moment, then I chirped up to Lucy again, "So, what's Victoria like?" I asked, thinking about Henry and his mother.

"It's so pretty there. I think you'd like it. Anyone should go there at least once in their lives."

I made an awkward face, somewhere between a smile and a smirk as I was increasingly interested in my new acquaintance.

"How long do you have to wait?" I inquired.

"About..." She trailed off, looking towards the clock. "thirty to forty minutes."

"Why don't we grab a coffee while we wait."

"Perfect, I'm in!"

"OK. Give me a few minutes while I take this to the Lost and Found."

I left my bag beside the bench and carried off Henry's suitcase alongside me. Once I arrived, I placed it on the floor while a couple inquired about their lost items. As I waited, I made the mistake of turning back to get a good look at Lucy. She was studying me as well, which caused me to turn away to see a tourist sign for Victoria. I eyeballed it so long that my vision became fuzzy as I zoned out.

"Sir?" The woman behind the counter spoke to me.

"Yes?" I replied, turning towards her.

"Do you have a claim?" Her tone was firm and businesslike.

I felt a surge of confusion, "A what?"

"Are you claiming a lost item," she clarified firmly, growing impatient.

I lifted the suitcase onto the counter, hesitating for a moment before responding. "I . . ." I began, but then glanced back at Lucy, who was now idly inspecting her nails.

“I’ll be right back,” I muttered, snatching the suitcase from the counter and hurrying back to where Lucy was sitting.

"Hey, you!"

She furrowed her brow as she looked back at me, "What happened?"

"Gotta question for ya! You mind taking me to an address in Victoria? I need to deliver this. I think it's best if I do it personally. I’ll pay for half of the gas.”

11:00 am

It was a good thing I called Cameron to tell him I was heading to Victoria; he wasn’t even out of bed when we spoke on the phone. It sounded like he completely forgot I was even coming. He pretended that it was because he was half-asleep, but my gut told me that he simply forgot. I was disappointed but relieved at the same time; this allowed me to spend more time with my new companion, Lucy, and hand deliver Henry’s suitcase to his mother.

I put two layers of sweaters on as the ferry took us across to Vancouver Island. It allowed the both of us to get to know one another. I discovered she had a large family: four brothers and two sisters. Much like me, she didn’t know her father, but her uncle always made a point of inviting her and her siblings over each summer, though only Lucy made the journey. She studied photography in college and found her way into the financial world; however, she still had a vibrant passion for photography.

I broke the silence that settled between us, "I'm guessing we are about the same age."

"Well, how old do you think I am?" Lucy asked, arching an eyebrow in curiosity.

"Same as me. I'm twenty-one,"

A wry smile played at the corner of her lips, "I'm twenty-three," Lucy confessed.

"Really?"

"Everyone thinks I'm younger than I am. Believe me, it works against me most of the time."

"Hmm."

I watched as Lucy's ponytail whipped back and forth in the wind. With her head turned to the ocean, I took advantage of the moment to admire her lovely profile. I enjoyed her mannerisms as she placed her hand over the rails of the ferry, peering out at the ocean. She appeared relaxed and content with what road life had paved for her thus far. She seemed to hold a maturity that I had yet to realize.

"Oh . . ." she chuckled to herself upon noticing my stare. "I know you want to deliver that luggage right away, but . . ."

I waited for her to continue.

"Would you mind if I went to my uncle's first? I want to let them know I'm OK, and I need to shower. I feel gross." Lucy asked.

"Of course."

"I just need like, thirty minutes."

I nodded in agreement.

3:00 pm

With my luggage still in the car and my new friend freshly showered, we drove to the address that I found in Henry's letter from his mother.

As I became more confident with myself, I explained to Lucy that I would stay at a motel and then get a cab back to the ferry the next day. The two of us exchanged numbers, mine was Cameron's and she gave me her uncle's, that way we could meet up the following week as planned.

"Turn right on Interurban Road," I instructed, my eyes fixed on the map spread out on my lap. "There it is, Interurban Road. Then turn onto Grange Road."

Lucy slowed the car as she approached the corner, her gaze shifting between the road ahead and my directions.

"There," I said, pointing towards the upcoming intersection. "Grange Road. Take a right."

I bobbed my head back and forth in anticipation as Lucy followed my guidance, maneuvering the car onto Grange Road.

"There!" I exclaimed, "Take a right here."

Lucy glanced at the house as she drove past, her eyes scanning the driveway, "There's a car in the driveway," she observed. "I'll stop here. Make sure it's the right house."

I nodded in agreement. Grabbing Henry's suitcase, I swung open the car door and stepped out onto the pavement. "OK," I replied as I made my way towards the house, the weight of the suitcase heavy in my hand.

The yard was surrounded by tall cedar trees. The driveway was gravel with an impressive looking sky-blue colored Cadillac with an Alberta license plate. I assumed it belonged to family visiting. Still carrying the suitcase, I turned to view the bumper of Lucy's rental. I continued up the steps of the modest-sized house; a story and a half building with bright white aluminum siding and a beautiful bay window. After giving the door a knock, I cleared my throat and took a step back.

After what seemed like two minutes, I placed the suitcase on the wooden porch and knocked again.

"Hmmm," I said and turned to look at the blue Cadillac. I leaned over to peer into the bay window to view several bouquets in it. I began to worry that I just wasted Lucy's time bringing me here, since it appeared no one was home. I gave the door another firm knock.

“Excuse me,” a woman’s voice called from next door. “They all gone.” The woman had a strong Hungarian accent.

“Pardon me?” I said, taking a few steps down.

“They all at the funeral home.”

“Oh.”

“Are you family?” she gently probed.

“No . . .” I hesitated. I suddenly felt awkward. “I met Henry on the train. They forgot his suitcase.” I explained, gesturing towards the porch as I spoke. Then, overcome by a sudden impulse, I added, “Do you know how he died? Was it a heart attack?”

“No.” The woman waddled towards me. “Brain aneurysm. It burst while he sleep. Very sad.”

I stood motionless, absorbing the news in silence.

“Bring here. You can leave it. I give it to Grace.” The woman offered, gesturing towards the suitcase.

“Ummm.” I stammered, feeling a surge of anxiety as I lurched towards the porch and snatched the suitcase. “Just a minute. I think there’s something else in the car.”

I raced back to the rental as I clutched the suitcase in my grasp.

"Hey," Lucy called out as I approached. "What happened?

"Shhh. Hold on." I whispered, my voice urgent as I flipped the suitcase open and quickly pulled out Henry's letter to Angie. "Hold on to this. Don't read it please." I instructed, pressing the letter into Lucy's hands.

"OK."

I slammed the suitcase shut and scurried back to the porch, where the neighbor was studying me curiously.

"There you go. A piece of clothing had fallen out on the way." I lied, handing over the suitcase and forcing a polite smile. "Tell his mother that I'm sorry."

"What your name?" Her accent was thick and heavy.

"It's Thomas. She never met me. Tell her . . . I liked Henry. He was a nice man," I reiterated.

I watched the woman nod in understanding and give me a polite wave before heading towards her house with Henry's suitcase.

I walked back to the car where Lucy sat with concern still etched across her face, her eyebrows were knit together. "Would you tell me what's going on?"

"Start the car, please. I'll explain on the way."

"Thomas?" Her tone was gentle yet insistent.

I turned to face her, "Yes?"

"What's in the letter?"

Chapter 12 (Thomas)

I waited outside the car and all the blood in my body rushed into my heart and my head. Lucy went inside to explain the situation to her aunt and uncle. Moments later, the front door swung open, and the three of them emerged.

"Oh, you poor man," Lucy's aunt exclaimed and she took my hand in her own. You've had some terrible luck. My name is Betty, and this is my husband Leonard."

"Let me grab your bag," Uncle Leonard offered.

7:00 pm

I felt so much better after having four days worth of grime and oil and even death washed off of me after my shower at Lucy's uncle's place. They agreed to have me there for two days and would drive me back to the ferry on Thursday.

After dinner, the two of us sat side by side on the couch in the basement where I gave a full narrative of Henry's story of his father, his affair with Cindy, and more specifically, his story of Angie Peterson. It was only then that I let her read the letter.

Lucy looked at me, then the letter, "So mister, whatcha gonna do with the letter?"

My voice was firm with determination, "I think I'm going to try and find her."

Lucy curled her top lip in skepticism. “How are you going to do that? There’s no address on it.”

“Yeah. I know. I’ll figure it out,” I murmured, my exhaustion evident in my voice as I let my head rest against the back of the sofa. “Somehow.”

I was exhausted. I felt my eyelids droop as weariness washed over me. I was pleasantly surprised when Lucy cupped my hand in hers and rested it on her lap, her touch offering a small comfort in the midst of my exhaustion.

"You're really tired, I can tell."

“I’m drained, emotionally and physically,” I admitted, taking a peek down at our hands that were intertwined on her lap.

I let out a small, almost silent breath. I stared up at the ceiling for a moment before caressing my thumb against her palm. They were baby smooth and soft. I turned my head to look at her sitting next to me. “Your hands are really soft,” I added with fatigue in my voice, I must've sounded intoxicated. My eyes were nearly closing with every breath.

"Mhm..." She added breathily. “Close your eyes,” Lucy instructed softly.

I obeyed. Her warm delicate caress was the ticket to my drifting off. The couch shifted when she moved, followed by a peck on my cheek which, surprisingly, didn’t wake me.

I lay there, eyes still closed, imagining the fields upon fields of wheat blowing in the wind. It was satisfyingly calm. I strode along the endless wheat fields, for what seemed like such a long time. The breeze was strong but beautiful as it ruffled my pants and shirt and blessed my face with the afternoon sun. The field opened up and far off in the distance was an object in the middle of it. *What is that? Go and see. Open it!* I rushed towards it at a walk, a quick pace, and finally a full stride until I was finally in front of it, a rectangular object. It's a suitcase. *Open it! Click*! *What is this? A letter. It's addressed to Angie*. *Crack*! *There it goes.* The wind took it. *Go after it. Run!* It blew away, far, far away, so far away that the little white envelope turned into a small white spec until it faded into oblivion.

Suddenly I exclaimed aloud, "Angie!" my eyes shot open and I jolted awake. Poking my head up, I looked to scan the dark basement I had been in for hours.

"Wh-What?" I scanned my surroundings. "Oh... Just- Just a dream." I sighed.

Wednesday, August 19th -- 8:30 am

During those initial five minutes, your senses slowly come alive before you fully awaken. In this case, I sensed the smell of freshly brewed coffee. I immediately imagined Henry sitting across from me, presenting me with a Styrofoam cup.

I was no longer on the train anymore. He was gone and the knot in my stomach began to form.

I turned to sit on the sofa, holding on to the edges of the cushions, taking deep breaths in and out to control my sudden onset of anxiety.

"You awake?" Lucy's voice echoed through the basement door as she poked her head in. “Are you OK?”

“I’m fine. I’ll be right up,” I replied, my voice groggy with sleep.

“You want coffee?” she offered.

"Please."

Her voice carried a hint of morning cheer, something I definitely wasn't used to, “How do you like it?”

“Cream and sugar.”

‘I hope you like cream and sugar,’ Henry would say as he passed the cup of coffee to me.

Why is that memory so fresh in my mind?

I rubbed my hands over my face a few times before I decided it was time to get up, so I got up from the couch and finally got dressed.

When I arrived at the breakfast table, the sun was brilliantly shining through Uncle Leonard’s kitchen window.

“Good morning,” he expressed, his legs crossed, sitting with the morning paper blocking his face. The back page flopped awkwardly as if it had been cut.

"There's sausages for the two of you when you decide to eat," Aunt Betty said as she flipped through the TV Guide.

"Thank you." I turned to Lucy who was already sitting at the kitchen table sipping her coffee. "Good morning!"

"'Mornin'" She pushed a cup of coffee toward me, followed by a newspaper clipping. "My uncle thought you might want this."

It read: *Henry Philip Thomas.* It was his obituary. Although the image was him, it must have been a photo taken several years ago when his hair was still dark.

"I've been thinking about this . . . situation you're in, since I woke up this morning," she said before taking a sip of her morning beverage, her hands wrapped around the mug, her golden-brown eyes hovering just above its rim.

"What situation?"

"Well . . . more as to . . . why you decided to take on the task of finding Angie. Wouldn't his mother not know of her whereabouts?" She hesitated.

"He never told his mother about how he left her," I explained quietly.

"Oh..." She fell silent, blowing on her coffee before taking another sip.

"He confessed to me that he never told his mother about leaving Angie with a child. I felt the need to, I don't know, still honor that I suppose." I shrugged, looking everywhere but her golden eyes.

She didn't respond which caused me to doubt if I did the right thing by stealing the letter. *Maybe I should not have snooped into Henry's suitcase in the first place.*

I felt uncertain and it was obvious, "Should I mail it back to her?"

Lucy shook her head, her silky brown hair swaying gently as she lowered her cup onto the table. "I think you should visit her while you're here," she suggested.

"What for?" I questioned, puzzled by her suggestion.

"The letter says something about his mother asking 'What ever happened to that Angie girl,' right?

"Well, yeah."

"Well," she continued, lifting the mug to her mouth, "maybe she'll know where to find her."

I leaned back in my chair, contemplating the task ahead while I absentmindedly tapped my fingertips on the tabletop.

"Come back next week," Uncle Leonard interjected, breaking the silence. "Let things settle for a bit."

Lucy lifted her eyebrows, her mug still situated in front of her as she grinned mischievously.

Chapter 13 (Thomas)

Tuesday, August 25th -- 1:20 pm

I discovered a couple of things in those seven days I spent at my childhood friend's place in Vancouver, like how people change a lot from when they were ten to when they turned twenty-one; Cameron was no exception. I'm not exactly sure as to what I was expecting, but my host turned into a party animal and did nothing but work, sleep, and party. I was disappointed to learn that he hadn't taken any time off from work as he had promised when we originally made plans for me to come.

Secondly, I came to the conclusion that I believe in fate. Although disappointed by my visit with Cameron, I wouldn't have had the opportunity to have met Henry or George the Barber. If I didn't meet Henry, I wouldn't have been moved to another car where I met George. If I hadn't met George, I wouldn't have received that haircut on the platform. If I hadn't received that haircut on the platform, Lucy wouldn't have approached me at the station. So yes, I *do* believe in fate.

My luck further changed when Lucy's aunt and uncle agreed to take me in as their guest for the remainder of my second week of vacation. So there I was, disembarking the ferry into Victoria Harbor, giving Lucy a wave of acknowledgment.

"Hi," I called out in casualty while placing my travel bag on the grass. Lucy stalked towards me with excitement, she opened her arms and wrapped them around me in a warm hug.

"Hello," she whispered as her head was perched over my shoulder.

"Can I tell you somethin'?" I expressed with my cheek pressed into the top of her head.

"What's that?" She whispered, squeezing me a little.

"Seeing you has been the best part of my trip."

"Really?" Her eyes sparkled as I nodded. "You know what?"

"What?"

She remained silent. Instead, I felt her body raise against mine, and the bottom of her feet rose. Her face tilted slightly to the left and she looked between my left eye, my right eye, and then my lips. Her non-verbal communication wasn't clear to me at first. I wasn't great at reading it at that point, but I eventually understood and went in for the kiss. The cherub lips were as beautiful to kiss as they looked. I don't know what took me so long.

I grabbed my bag with one hand and her hand with the other.

"I take it you didn't enjoy your visit with Cameron all that much?"

I expressed that I was a little disappointed in someone who used to be a close friend. However, people change. He grew up and so did I. We had nothing in common anymore. I was bored silly while sitting in his apartment and it was sad to think that I probably wouldn't see him again, but that's life.

"Oh, that's unfortunate about your friendship, but I'm glad we met, y'know. I'll still be around for another two weeks after you're gone."

"That's a nice vacation for you," I said, placing my bag in the back seat, hiding my disappointment at learning I would be traveling back home without her by my side.

"You're planning to call Mrs. Thomas this afternoon, aren't you?"

"Yes, Lucy."

3:30 pm

I gently placed the receiver back onto the phone's cradle, exhaling softly as I turned back to Lucy.

"So, are you all set for tomorrow?" Lucy asked with excitement as she held her crossed fingers beside her head.

"Yes, I am. She seems nice, Mrs. Thomas."

"So..."

"I don't think I'll bring it up," I confessed, shaking my head. "I mean, I'll mention Angie, but I just can't bring myself to tell her about Angie being pregnant."

"Fine, I guess I see your point," Lucy conceded, playfully slapping my knee as she leaned back in her chair.

Later on, while on the basement sofa which was also my bed, I realized something. It was strange but Lucy reminded me of the image Henry had given me of Angie Peterson.

"What are you looking at me like that for?" Lucy asked, raising an eyebrow as she caught my gaze. "You hoping for some action or something? They're just upstairs," she teased, pointing upwards with her finger.

"No, that wasn't it," I replied.

"An ex?" Lucy guessed. She leaned in closer, awaiting my response.

"No." I shook my head. I decided to keep it to myself. Even though it made *me* happy, it would have been inappropriate to tell her, so I changed the subject.

"You're going to come in with me, aren't you?"

"What are you talkin' about?"

"Mrs. Thomas. You're coming in with me, right?"

"If you want me to."

Wednesday, August 26th -- 12:00 pm

"Hello, Mrs. Thomas," My voice was slightly shaky with nerves and I shifted on my feet. "Um, I hope you don't mind. This is my friend, Lucy," I introduced, gesturing towards her.

"Oh . . ." At first, Henry's mother seemed irritated, but she eventually waved dismissively. "Don't be silly. I need the company. Come in. Come in," she said, pulling the door towards her slight figure.

Mrs. Thomas was a frail woman who was in her late seventies. She was slightly hunched, her face was thin and dotted with age spots, and she had stark white hair that appeared to be freshly curled.

"Please," she gestured with her tiny arm. "Have a seat." The woman followed us to the living room, where a cuckoo clock ticked loudly.

The house held an unusual fragrance of cedar wood and mothballs.

I was caught by surprise by my sudden inability to start the conversation. So instead of speaking, I studied the clock's pendulum swinging back and forth behind its chains. Above the clock face was a little door that housed something that frightened me as much as a horror movie.

"Do you like cuckoo clocks?" Mrs. Thomas asked, following my eyes to the fixture on the wall.

“I do.” I lied with a nod. Cuckoo clocks scared the shit out of me when that stupid little bird poked its head out unannounced.

“I think they’re crazy!” Lucy added with a nervous chuckle. “But I think they’re pretty cool. I like ‘em.”

Our host forced a grin and rocked back in her chair slightly before asking, “Would you like tea?”

Lucy and I replied at the same time, which was when Mrs. Thomas pushed herself off the chair. “I’ll put the kettle on, then,” she muttered as she shuffled into the nearby kitchen.

Moments later, she returned, placing a plate of cookies on the center table.

“I hope you like Peek Freans. I don’t have young people as guests very often.”

“I like the ones with the little jelly in the middle,” I said, eyeing the plate.

Mrs. Thomas clasped the plate tenuously with her bent fingers. The rheumatoid arthritis in her hand was so severe that her fingers were nearly deformed. She presented the mound of cookies, “Please, take one.”

I bit into mine which brought back memories of my childhood.

“Before I forget,” the elderly woman began. “I wanted to thank you for bringing Henry’s suitcase. That was an honorable thing to do. Yet . . ." She lifted her boney finger to scratch her chin. "I don't quite understand how you two met. You are so much younger. I can't imagine what you'd two have in common."

Lucy and I glanced at each other quickly before I answered. There was a reason for that indiscreet look as she had convinced me to bring the letter. I had agreed under the condition that if I felt the situation warranted it, I would explain everything to his mother, otherwise I would stay silent on the topic of his leaving Angie with child.

"Well, Henry and I met on the train when we boarded in Toronto." I paused before continuing. "He mentioned something a day or two before he . . . uh . . . passed. He mentioned a woman named Angie Peterson. Did he ever mention her to you?"

The frail woman held her hands between her knees whilst she listened to the inquiry. She eventually nodded, saying, "Henry mentioned her a few times. He even wrote to me from her house when they lived together. Then . . ." she paused and let her eyes roam the living room. "Before I knew it. He was at my doorstep. Didn't bring a thing with him except the clothes on his back. Well . . . I had figured something had happened between them. A breakup of some sorts, maybe. What exactly, I'm not sure."

When Mrs. Thomas shook her head, it continued a little too long, which I determined to be involuntary. "I asked him about it once, but it seemed to really upset him, so I never brought it up again." The woman shrugged her shoulders and paused again. "I'm surprised her name came up. He must have told you an awful lot."

Her head began shaking once again. "He never told anybody much about anything. Almost makes me wonder if he knew he was going to die." Mrs. Thomas murmured in sadness. She glanced away for a moment.

She turned to me. "What did he say about his old... fling?"

I struggled with how much I would tell her and thought about what Lucy had said. But when I reached for the letter that was tucked in my back pocket, my friend grabbed my arm and held it down, pretending it to be an endearing gesture, but her squeeze hurt a little.

"He wanted to say how much he still cared for her," Lucy interjected. ". . . and regretted breaking up with her. Thomas lives in Ajax and wanted to pass along the message to her personally. Ajax and Whitby are practically next to each other. Do you happen to have her address?"

"Oh, dear." The white-haired woman stood while slapping her knees. "I have some of his letters in my hutch. Let me find my glasses and . . ." the woman's voice trailed off as she shifted down the hallway.

I released my arm from Lucy's grip, rubbing it to soothe the sensation of her firm grasp. "What did you do that for?" I whispered, trying to keep my voice low.

"Shhh! I'll explain later. Don't you dare pull that letter out!" Lucy hushed while her eyes darted around to make sure Mrs. Thomas wasn't around.

I was surprised by her sudden change of heart. I was certain she wanted me to divulge Henry's secret to his mother.

Mrs. Thomas mumbled something in the other room but neither of us could make it out, so we just waited for the woman to emerge, which she eventually did.

"I found it," she said, waddling over to us. "I brought a pad and pencil for you to write it down."

I was ecstatic. I could hardly contain my nerves, but I needed to keep things in perspective as the woman had just lost her son, so I stifled my delight and said, "Thank you. I think this would make him happy."

While I wrote the address, I noticed Lucy reach over and place her hand lovingly on Mrs. Thomas's knee.

"I'm so sorry," she said and passed her a tissue.

"It's still not real to me. I still feel like he's going to show up at my doorstep one day, just like he's done so many times before."

I raised my head to regard the grieving woman. Even though I empathized, I must admit I felt completely helpless. Thank goodness Lucy was with me. I'm not sure how I would have handled it well by myself if I had done it alone.

While studying my chicken-scratch writing on the notepad, I heard the kettle whistle, which was when Mrs. Thomas straightened her back and slapped her hands on her lap, "Anyway. There's lots of time for tears. Now it's time for tea."

"Let me help you," Lucy offered with a polite smile, following their hostess into the kitchen.

As I sat alone, it occurred to me that the likelihood of finding this woman at the given address was fairly low. *People move, Tommy-boy. What the hell makes you think this woman would still be there after twenty years?*

I jumped in my seat when the cuckoo bird flew out of its door to chime one o'clock. I would have expressed a loud obscenity if it wasn't for the company I was with.

"I love it," Lucy softly laughed as she re-entered the living room.

Chapter 14 (Thomas)

On the way home from Mrs. Thomas's, Lucy had told me as to why she thought it wasn't the best idea to reveal Henry's letter to his mother. She explained that Mrs. Thomas had suffered enough and that there was no guarantee that I would even find Angie Peterson. Furthermore – as Lucy detailed – even if we did find this woman, she could have possibly miscarried, given the child up or lost the baby, which would have become an even greater loss for the elderly woman.

My new companion helped prepare me for my mission to locate Miss Peterson upon my return, as I intended to do so after my arrival. We discussed several scenarios, but we both agreed that if Henry was twenty-five when he lived with his former lover, the year would have been 1961. He ended up leaving in the fall of that same year, at which point she would have been two to three months pregnant and would have given birth, if the child survived, in the year 1962. The child, or rather, teenager, would be nineteen years old. The address that Henry's mother gave was on Anderson St. in Whitby, Ontario. It was worth a shot.

The train ride back to Toronto seemed to pass quicker even though it was far less eventful than my journey to the west coast. Considering the fact that I often attempted to make new acquaintances along the way, everyone that I made eye contact with or said hello to just kept to themselves. Perhaps my return to Toronto was natural and what I experienced on the way to Vancouver was supernatural. I suppose I'll never know the answer to that question.

Thursday, September 3rd -- 2:00 pm

"Where are you going? You just got back!" my mother called from the kitchen as I hurriedly slipped into my shoes.

"I'm just going to apply to a few places," I remarked casually.

My mother turned the corner to see me getting ready to leave, "You got copies of your resume?"

"Right here," Reaching into my bag, I pulled out a near stack of resumes.

My mother was in her early forties. She had gray eyes with pronounced crow's feet on either side; something I never really noticed until I returned from Vancouver. She had just finished the dishes, and while still wearing her rubber gloves and apron, she asked, "Why don't you wait five minutes and I'll give you a drive? This is my only day off this week."

"It's OK. I kind of want to do this on my own."

"Suit yourself."

* * *

It took just over an hour for the bus to drop me at Taunton and Anderson. Anderson Street stretched for about a quarter of a mile before it sloped upwards.

The afternoon sun was beaming down on the back of my neck as I made the trek along the desolate road. Anderson Street was mostly fields and cedar trees, peppered with the odd house. The sound of the traffic on Taunton Road diminished the closer I approached the incline.

As I continued to the top, there emerged a brick farmhouse with a dilapidated barn and an overgrown field. On the opposite side of the road was a small house with gray aluminum siding—a Ford Fiesta parked in the dirt driveway. The house was rather drab looking but I was excited nonetheless

"This is it," I said to myself.

I had practiced what I was going to say when I met that acclaimed woman, but I didn't anticipate being this nervous when the time came. To make matters worse, I had difficulty imagining Angie as a forty-five-year-old woman. I couldn't get the idea out of my head that she would look like Lucy. It was somehow ingrained in my mind since I met Lucy that morning in Vancouver. *No Tommy-boy, she's forty-five and looks nothing like Lucy.*

I raised my hand to knock. I backed away from the door, took another deep breath, and waited. After a few moments, I heard rustling behind the screen door before it opened. On the other side of it was a teenage girl with messy hair and an abundance of pimples. She was about my height and very shy. *Could this be Henry's daughter?*

"Uh . . . can I help you?" The teenage girl questioned as she peered at me through the screen door.

"Hi. Is . . . is your mother home?" I hesitated.

"Yeah. Hold on," The girl turned and let the screen door slam shut behind her.

"Mom," I heard her call from inside. "Some guy's at the door wanting to talk to you," she announced.

I felt my body tremble with anticipation, I would finally get to meet the woman I'd thought so much about and had become so determined to meet. It also occurred to me that no matter how much I wanted to pass along Henry's message, I could be negatively disrupting someone's life at the cost of a dead man's wish. Not only was it *his* wish, but it became *my* fascination.

“Yes?” a young woman answered.

I was so stunned by my previous thoughts I froze and couldn't muster a word, even though I knew it wasn't Angie Peterson.

“Is there something you wanted?” the woman repeated.

The woman on the other side of the door was in her thirties and was wearing what looked like a work uniform of some kind.

“I’m sorry to bother,” I managed to stammer out finally, my voice sounding feeble and uncertain. “I was looking for someone who used to live here.”

“Well, I moved here a couple of years ago,” the woman replied while peering at me through the doorway.

“I see.” I felt foolish as the event just confirmed how futile the entire exercise had been. “The person I’m looking for lived here . . . twenty years ago.”

“Good Lord!” she chuckled. “I can’t help you with that. You’d have to talk to the previous owner.”

“OK.” I stepped away. “Again, sorry to bother you.”

I turned towards the road.

“He lives right there,” the woman said. She had stepped out of her door to point across the street at the farmhouse.

“The old farmer. He’s the one that sold it to me.”

A sense of relief washed over me, "Really? Thank you."

I made quick strides along the dirt driveway of the farmhouse that was nestled between several large Maple trees. *Maybe my luck had just turned around.*

“Hello there,” a voice called near the barn. “What can I do for ya?”

The farmer came around from his tractor wearing faded work pants and a plaid shirt, sporting a John Deere cap.

He appeared to be in his seventies and was severely hunched.

“I just came from across the street. The lady there said you owned that house at one time,” I began, shifting nervously as I approached the man and his tractor.

“What’s this all about?” he asked, his brow furrowing slightly as he leaned on his tractor, studying me intently.

“I was looking for someone who lived there twenty years ago. Her name was Angie Peterson,”

“Are you the police or somethin’? You don’t look like a cop,” the man replied, his skepticism evident in his voice as he squinted at me, waiting for my response.

“No sir. A fr- a friend of mine was wondering where she may have moved to. He said it was twenty years ago, so 1961. Somewhere around then.”

“I don’t want no trouble. Can you. . .” The man turned and called to his front door. “Martha.” He waited for an answer. “Martha?” he repeated.

“What?” a woman’s voice snapped from inside the house.

“Come out here a minute.” He echoed back to her.

A woman in her sixties with wiry gray hair entered the porch wearing very baggy jeans and a pink and yellow blouse.

“Well, hi there,” she greeted me. “What’s going on, Burt?” She turned to her husband, then back at me.

"This guy's asking about a woman who lived at that place we sold a couple of years ago. What's her name?"

"Angie Peterson."

"Angie Peterson." He squinted again. "I do remember a girl there," he said, turning to his wife.

"Yup," the woman replied. "A lovely girl. Gave us no trouble. What business you got looking for her? She's long gone from 'ere." She stepped off her porch.

"Would you happen to know where she lives now?" I asked, trying not to sound desperate.

The woman chuckled. "That was ages ago. I've got no clue. Are you a relative?"

"No. It's kind of a long story. There's a man I met who knew her and wanted to pass along a message."

"Then . . ." the woman turned to her husband. "Why doesn't he do that himself?" she asked harshly.

The husband nodded in agreement, crossing his arms.

"Because . . . he died a couple of weeks ago."

"Oh, for goodness's sake," the woman peered up at the sky, then back to me. "Sometimes it's best to leave the past in the past—I always say, right Burt?"

The farmer nodded and sucked his teeth.

"OK," I backed down. "Sorry to disturb you."

"Good day to ya," the woman waved.

* * *

As I made the trek down the incline of Anderson Street, I felt defeated and even foolish for thinking that I could find a woman who lived at a residence some twenty years earlier. I always knew the probability was low, but based on what the outcome was, I felt utterly ridiculous. Still, there was one more avenue I hadn't explored.

5:00 pm

"OK. Thank you." I hung up the phone with an agitated huff. That was the last of the A. Peterson's of the Ajax, Whitby, Oshawa, and Bowmanville phone directory.

Well. That's it, Tommy-boy. There's nothing else you can do now. Just chalk it up as defeat and move on. Look at the bright side, you met Lucy! That was a positive.

Chapter 15 (Thomas)

Wednesday, September 9th -- 6:00 pm

Another week went by and although I resigned myself to the fact that the search for Henry's ex-lover was over, I hadn't quite forgotten about it. It was still in the back of my mind. I had debated telling Mother about meeting him, but I didn't. I'm not sure why. I think it was because I felt it to be a private matter. Furthermore, she had become a little nosey as of late, which annoyed me.

"So, Mister Thomas Henry, you got a letter today," she said, holding a small envelope in her hand. "It's from a *Lucy Kowalski*, from Victoria." She grinned before placing it on the table in front of me. "Who is this Lucy girl? I thought you spent your vacation with Cameron." She crossed her arms as she looked at me.

"Let me see it," I said, studying the perfectly printed envelope which was too thick and heavy to contain just a plain letter.

"What happened to you on that trip anyway?" she continued to prod. "You're not yourself. You've changed, I think." She pressed her lips together in annoyance.

"Nothing, Mom," I dismissed as I plopped myself onto the living room couch and carefully opened the envelope. Out came a folded letter and three, color photos: one of a giant tree, one of the Vancouver skyline, and one of old totem poles—all of which looked professionally taken.

The letter read:

Hello, Ontario boy! Ha Ha Ha. Greetings from Victoria! I hope your ride back was uneventful. I thought I'd send you a quick note to let you know what I've been up to. Uncle Leonard and Aunt Betty took me to The Charlottes, which is a group of islands up the coast, which had these very historic totem poles. I used about four rolls of film there (I added one just for you). We also went to Stanley Park for a day as well, but the highlight of my trip so far was, (besides meeting you of course), visiting The Charlottes.

Besides my interest in photography, I took up jogging with my uncle. I think I'm going to run more when I get back home. I'm addicted now!!

I'd ask you to write me back, but by the time you get this, I will be boarding the train back home, so I will call you when I get back into the city. I'm looking forward to hearing all about your adventures in finding Miss Angie.

Kisses,

Lucy.

Mother wandered into the living room as I hastily tucked the pictures and letter back into the envelope. "Well, are you going to tell me about this girl?" she inquired, peeking over the couch. "Too bad she lives so far away."

"She lives in Scarborough. So not far at all."

“Oh,” she raised her eyebrows. “It’s like pulling teeth with you. Are you going to tell me how you met?” Her face suddenly changed. “C’mon, Thomas. Is it an older woman or something?”

“No, Mom. Stop it! She’s my age. Well . . . technically. She’s two years older, but she looks younger than twenty-three,” I explained, frustration edging into my voice.

“And?”

“We met when the train arrived in Vancouver. I . . .”

She waited for me to elaborate, “Yes?”

“I ended up spending a couple of nights with her at her uncle’s place on the Island.”

"What?! You slept with a girl you just met?”

“Jesus, Mom. No. Her uncle and aunt invited me over. I stayed in the basement,” I said as I sauntered towards the kitchen. “Can I have a beer?” I asked, eyeing the fridge hopefully.

“So long as you pour me a small glass,” She followed me to the kitchen and leaned against the island. “So. Her name is Lucy,” Mother continued, her tone thoughtful as she processed the information. “And she lives in Toronto.”

I poured Mother a glass of beer and held onto the bottle. I nodded and took a swig of my beer, “She leaves for home on . . . Friday. She’ll be back home Tuesday,” I took a hopeful inhale, "I'd like to invite her over for the weekend when she arrives."

Her eyebrow rose. Her pensive look was not reassuring.

"Mom. I think you're forgetting I'm twenty-one."

"I'm aware of that. But what about- What about her parents? Would they have a problem with it?"

"She lives with her mom too. She's like twenty-three. I hardly think her mom would have an issue with it."

She let out a long sigh. "I suppose there's no harm in it. Besides, I'd like to meet this . . . *Lucy Kowalski.*"

Saturday, September 12th -- 2:00 pm

"OK, now clutch in," Lucy instructed, her voice calm and patient. "Down to second. Let the clutch out . . . Ugh!" Her head bobbed against the passenger seat. "OK. A little slower next time."

I felt a pang of frustration as I grabbed the wheel again, "Sorry, Lucy."

"It's OK. Once you get used to the sweet spot, it will be easier. OK. Now, again, your RPMs are high, so clutch in. Bring it up into third . . . Yeah. There you go. That was smooth," Lucy encouraged, her tone brightening as she saw improvement.

I've driven my mother's car many times but never driven a car with a manual transmission. I kind of liked it, even though I stalled it a few times. My instructor was incredibly patient, which made the experience even better.

"OK. Now fourth . . . there, even better."

"I'm going to pull in here and let you take over," I said as I slowed the vehicle into a vacant parking lot where I stalled it by trying to gear-down.

"Just leave it off," she said and straightened herself in the passenger seat. "So, I still don't understand. Why haven't you told your mom about Henry and your search?" Lucy reached over and casually tousled the back of my hair, her touch gentle and comforting.

I hadn't thought about either for the last week. I pushed it out of my head for the simple fact that my mission had failed and there was little-to-no hope of finding Angie Peterson. The only comforting thing was that when I thought of Angie, I immediately imagined seeing Lucy. So never finding this woman was not a bad thing. Perhaps the real Angie Peterson would have ruined that mindset.

"Because it's done anyway," I blurted. "There's no chance of finding her." I looked at Lucy and then out of the front windshield. "And you know what . . . there's nothing I can do about it. I tried. If anything, I feel sad about the fact that I couldn't give Mrs. Thomas a call and let her know that she has a grandchild. And really, what's the point of telling my mom anyway? She'll just make a big issue out of it."

Lucy continued twisting and playing with the hair at the back of my neck, brushing her fingers against my skin every so often. "OK. I understand. It would just be like . . . a build-up over a non-event. I get it." Her words soothed me.

"Yeah," I concluded as I got out and rounded the vehicle. I pulled the passenger door open for Lucy but she didn't attempt to get out. She remained stationary as an unusual-looking grin spread across her face.

I was intrigued by her sudden change in expression, "What?"

"Nothing," she replied coyly, but her grin widened.

I prodded and a giggle escaped my lips, "What?"

"Have I ever told you that you have a very unique nose?" she asked, her tone teasing. "It's very . . . I don't know . . . distinguished."

My brows knit together, "Distinguished?"

"Yeah," she confirmed, nodding thoughtfully. "I like it. It's . . ." She paused, squinting as if searching for the right words. ". . . very Jacque Cousteau looking."

"Ummm . . ." I let out a chuckle, "okay,"

"It's a compliment, don't worry," she reassured me, flashing me another grin before hopping over the center console and into the driver's seat. "Come on, Tommy. Let's go for a detour."

4:00 pm

"Where did you two go?" Mother asked when we arrived. "I was wondering if you were ever coming back. I didn't want dinner to sit too long."

"Lucy was showing me how to drive stick."

I realized the innuendo right after I said it, so I quickly turned away from my girlfriend to avoid an outburst of laughter.

6:00 pm

After dinner, Lucy and I sat at the kitchen table, chatting with Mother, who was washing the dinner dishes.

"Want me to dry?" I offered, peering over at the sink where my mom, clad in a rubber apron and gloves, was finishing off the last of the dishes.

"No, no. There's not that much here," she replied, glancing out the kitchen window as she scrubbed. "I'm thinking of having a birthday party next weekend."

"Huh? Why? I just had mine in July,"

"I meant for me, silly. My birthday is this month."

"Oh," I replied sheepishly, feeling a flush of embarrassment. My girlfriend playfully scrunched her face and then unexpectedly pinched my side.

I yelped, taken aback by the sudden pinch.

“What are you two up to?” Mother asked as she continued to stare out the window, the birds still chirping. “Maybe Lucy would like to come by next weekend for that.” She paused. “I think I’ll invite your aunt Ange and Uncle Larry over too. I haven’t seen them in a while.”

“Sure,” I agreed, still taking in the thought of having my new girlfriend over again, but Lucy wasn’t smiling when I turned to face her.

“What’s wrong?” I whispered to her lowly.

She tilted her neck towards my mother. I wasn’t getting what she was indicating until she said: “Your aunt Ange,” she replied in a low voice. “Ange . . . Angie?” She continued stretching her neck.

“Mom?” I called while still maintaining eye contact with Lucy.

She looked back at me, “Yes, hon?”

“What was Aunt Ange’s last name before she married Uncle Larry?”

She stopped moving and tilted her head to one side as she thought. “Blake,” she casually mentioned and continued splashing in the sink.

“Oh.” *Another defeat for me*. Lucy turned to me, pouting.

"Want some blueberry pie?" I offered, turning to Lucy with a hopeful smile. "Mom made it just before you came."

"No," Mom interjected abruptly, standing motionless once more.

"What? How come?" I asked, taken aback by her sudden refusal. I couldn't tell if she was being serious or facetious.

“It’s not Blake,” she said, then angled her neck to speak, both of her hands were still immersed in the sink. “It’s Robertson . . . or something like that.”

Sunday, September 13th -- 1:30 pm

I still held my secret from Mother, which Lucy was vehemently opposed to, and made a point of it on our way to visit Aunt Ange and Uncle Larry.

The tension was thick between us as Lucy drove. I could tell she was annoyed with me. “I still don’t understand why you didn’t tell her in the first place. Imagine how it looks," She broke the silence, "me secretly driving you around to see if your aunt had a love child from twenty years ago."

We looked at each other and her expression softened as she turned to me.

"Because she wouldn't have let me go. She would have kiboshed the whole thing. Besides, I need to pass along this message. I . . . I can't believe it would be my aunt."

"Could be," she interjected thoughtfully.

"Yeah, exactly," I agreed, "That's why I didn't say anything."

"Fine," Lucy sighed, I could see her frustration in the way she tugged her fingers through her hair. "I still don't think it was right for you to call your aunt behind your mother's back."

"Anyway, you heard me," I continued, "Before I could come right out and ask her maiden name, she invited me over."

I never connected the name of my aunt to "Angie." She was always Aunt Ange to me. She wasn't my aunt by blood, but rather someone my mother knew for so long that I just ended up calling her Aunt Ange. A very close family friend.

I figured Aunt Ange to be about forty-five and Mother did tell me she lived in Whitby when they first met, so I was still hopeful. My aunt never had a child as far as I knew, so the chances of her being "the one" was also a long shot, but I needed to know.

Aunt Ange lived in Newcastle which was about an hour's drive from Ajax.

* * *

“Hello, Tommy!” Aunt Ange always called me “Tommy.” “And who is this young lady?” She greeted the both of us with a warm smile.

“This is my girlfriend, Lucy.”

“Nice to meet you. Come on in.” We followed Aunt Ange to the living room, where she already had sandwiches and a can of Coke set out for me. “I wasn’t expecting two of you, but the more, the merrier! Let me grab some biscuits and another pop for you, Lucy.” Aunt Ange hummed a tune while she searched the cupboards in her kitchen.

She returned with a plate of biscuits and another can of Coke, “Your uncle is out cutting the grass. He’ll be at it for a good hour.”

I studied my aunt’s face and the way she gracefully sat with her hands clasped together. *Is this the true Angie Peterson that Henry spoke of?*

"So, you met someone and you think they might know me?" Aunt Ange asked, her hands sliding between her knees as she maintained her composure, though a hint of tension lingered.

"Yes," I confirmed, "His name was Henry."

Aunt Ange visibly stiffened at the mention of the name, her posture becoming more upright as she processed the information. "Was?"

"Yes..." My voice faltered slightly as I recounted the events that took place on the train. "Well, as you know, I took the train to Vancouver last month. I met this man. We talked and talked for like... three days and then..." I hesitated, the memory still fresh in my mind. "He died... in his sleep."

Aunt Ange's gaze shifted away for a moment, her expression unreadable as she processed the news. It appeared she was upset.

I can't believe this! My aunt Ange is Angie Peterson!

"This is his obituary," I pulled the clipping from my pocket. "He was forty-five."

She studied the clipping for a moment before tilting her head slightly, "Ah... no. Your math is wrong. He was born in 1934. That makes him forty-seven. Well, he would have been forty-seven this month," Aunt Ange corrected as she handed back the newspaper clipping.

"Huh!"

"So, technically, he was forty-six when he died," she clarified "I do know a Henry from a long time ago, but... I don't know this man."

I turned to Lucy who sucked in her teeth at my latest failure.

"What's this all about, anyway?" Her gaze shifted between us as she scanned the puzzled look on my face. Lucy took the opportunity to explain the situation, detailing Angie's involvement, Henry's departure and abandoning his child, and the mysterious letter that had prompted our visit.

Aunt Ange's composed stare broke and before I knew it, the woman broke out laughing; she followed that with a playful slap on my knee.

"Really Tommy? Did you think I was part of that love movement of the sixties? I thought you knew me better than that. I was a straight-laced girl . . . and still am. That's hilarious," she snorted. "Come on. Let's eat and tell me how you two met.

* * *

"You know . . ." Lucy started, her eyes darted towards me.

"Don't!" I said firmly, "Please, not right now."

I felt utterly stupid and didn't want to talk about it. I needed silence, which Lucy granted while we drove back. The only exception was to let me know she was taking a detour.

"I'm turning here," she whispered, and I could see her hands turning the wheel.

I was confused by Lucy's change in direction, "Why?"

"Because I want to buy your mom something for having me over," Lucy replied with a smile.

"Okay." I leaned my head against the passenger window, gazing out into the passing scenery.

"Do you think your aunt will tell your mom?" Lucy's question brought me back to the present.

I pondered her inquiry for a moment before responding, "I don't know. I hope not."

Lucy reached over and placed her hand on my lap, offering a reassuring gesture. She then turned into a plaza that housed a flower shop, a bakery, and a hardware store.

"I'll be right back," she said, planting a hearty kiss on my cheek before getting out of the car.

"Mhm..."

As soon as the door shut, I felt bad for being so curt. It wasn't her fault my journey had failed and finally come to an end.

Aunt Ange having a love child, I thought to myself. *I* even chuckled at the thought. *Oh yeah. She's going to call Mom. I can just imagine it now. 'Thomas, can I speak with you for a minute please?' 'Yes, mom.'*

I rolled down the window to take in the fresh air, the afternoon sun perfectly positioned directly in front of me. That's when I determined that what I did was OK. That's when I discovered that not all things work out the way you had initially hoped. That's when I realized that Lucy was in the flower shop which was directly beside The Village Bake Shoppe! *I wonder.*

I hopped out of the car and made my way in, once inside I perused the long glass display cabinets, stealing glances up at the servers who were all well below the age of forty-five. *That one's like in her teens, that one's, thirty, thirty-five-ish. Nope! No forty-five-year-old.*

It was a cute little place. It had two large glass cabinets of wonderfully decorated cakes and other baked goods behind them. There were also a few small two-seater-type tables scattered about.

"Can I help you?" The young employee asked, looking me up and down.

"Ummmm . . ." I turned to see if Lucy was waiting for me. "Do you have any Black Forest cake?" I asked.

The woman lowered herself, examining the long cabinet before responding, "I think we're out. Hold on. Angie?" she called as she poked her head through the back. "Are we out of Black Forest?"

Moments later, a middle-aged woman emerged wearing a white apron, powder and icing were scattered on it.

"Sorry," the woman greeted me. "We're out right now. I can have one made for you?"

I studied Angie Peterson and how unalike she was compared to the image I had of her in my mind. However, it wasn't a disappointment. Her demeanor was pleasant and warm, reminiscent of visiting a family member I hadn't seen in years. All the while I deliberated, I lost the sense of time including my queue to speak, which was when she chuckled to herself and took a step closer. "Sir?" She repeated, trying to gain my attention.

"Yes?" I finally replied, my mind still processing the encounter.

"Is it . . . for an occasion?"

My thoughts raced, "Yes, yes it is... actually."

The woman cleared her throat before speaking, tilting her head slightly. "Excuse me, but . . . do I know you?"

I struggled to find my words. "Have you been here . . . like . . . a long time?"

The woman raised her eyebrow, followed by a half-grin. "Twenty-two years."

"Is your name Angie Peterson?"

The young employee beside her beamed at me, her eyes widened in disbelief at my directness. The young lady then scooted off to serve another customer.

"It *was*," she replied with a furrowed brow. "Ummm. . . you still didn't answer my question. Do I know you?" She pressed again.

I felt numb, my mind was going through a whirlwind of memories and emotions I had felt for nearly two months. Henry, his stories, George the barber, the letter, the regrets, the farmer and his wife—they all flashed through my mind in a chaotic jumble.

"No." I tried to gather the courage to meet the kind and serene eyes Henry had spoken of. "I think my mom went to high school with you."

Her expression softened, "Who's your mom?"

"Lesley Henry. Well... it used to be Lesley Bordon, but she got married."

She pursed her lips in thought, "I don't recall a Lesley Bordon. Doesn't ring a bell," she admitted, wiping her hands on her apron. "Is the cake for her?"

"Well then," Angie Peterson grabbed a pen from a cup beside the register and leaned over the counter. "So . . . Happy Birthday, Lesley? No . . . of course not. Happy Birthday, Mom, right?"

I peered over to view her pad, nodding in confirmation. "Yes. Can you have it ready for next weekend?"

"Of course! What's your name?" she asked, pen poised over the paper.

"Thomas," I replied, feeling a twinge of nervousness in my chest.

I studied Angie's face while she wrote. Although she was no longer the young woman ingrained in my mind for so long, I could somehow relate to the person on the other side of the counter. To me, she hadn't necessarily aged. Those crinkles around her eyes represented more than just years passed by. And she didn't have bitterness painted on her face like an aged piece of leather hung out in the blazing sun. No, this woman was content. She was at peace. She had already dealt with whatever happened and moved on. I don't why, but I assumed she wouldn't have.

Angie finally raised her head. "Have your mother come by for a visit sometime," the woman behind the counter called out. "I'm sure we have some common friends."

"OK. I will."

As I left The Village Bake Shoppe to greet Lucy, I heard the bell above the door chime softly behind me.

"What the hell? I thought you were still in the car. My keys were still in the ignition," Lucy exclaimed as I approached.

"Oh shit. Sorry," I muttered an apology, feeling a wave of exhaustion wash over me.

"What happened? You didn't buy any . . . holy! You're as white as a ghost! What the hell happened?"

"Nothing, Lucy. I guess I'm just really tired. I'll have a nap when we get back... I didn't sleep well last night." I tried to dismiss the unease creeping into my mind, "I ordered a birthday cake for mom . . . you know, for next weekend."

"Awe. That was sweet," Lucy said, giving my leg a comforting rub before starting the car.

* * *

On the ride home, I contemplated what had just happened. I typically would have regretted my decision earlier and demanded that Lucy turn back around —but I didn't. I never second-guessed my choice. I was confident with it.

It was a little strange, but it was somehow comforting knowing Angie Peterson was only the next town over. As I recollected the last few weeks, I realized that I had learned a lot on my trip to Vancouver. Not every story needs to be told. Not every secret needs to be unveiled. People make decisions for a reason. Understandably, they may regret them, but they made them just the same. I'm sure many would criticize me for the decision *I* made or do something different. But I didn't care.

As for the past; I can't change that. I thought I could, but once faced with the reality of it, it was like trying to haul up a sunken ship for answers. That's not always the right choice.

The farmer's wife was right. Sometimes it *is* best to leave the past in the past.

The End

This story is dedicated to George the Barber

Made in United States
North Haven, CT
02 March 2024